Zombie Diaries
Summer Break Junior Year
The Mavis Saga

By
R.W.K. Clark

Published in the United States by Clarkltd.
Po Box 45313 Rio Rancho, NM 87174
info@clarkltd.com

Edition 1

United States Copyright Office
#1-6140530652 Dec 2017
Library of Congress Control Number: 2017907165
International Standard Book Numbers
ISBN-10: 1948312034
ISBN-13: 978-1948312035
ASIN: B07H5PR2BS

/200801

ZOMBIE DIARIES SERIES

Zombie Diaries - Homecoming Junior Year - ZD1
ISBN-10: 0997876778 ISBN-13: 978-0997876772

Zombie Diaries - Winter Formal Junior Year - ZD2
ISBN-10: 0997876786 ISBN-13: 978-0997876789

Zombie Diaries - Prom Junior Year - ZD3
ISBN-10: 0997876794 ISBN-13: 978-0997876796

Zombie Diaries - Summer Break Junior Year - ZD4
ISBN-10: 1948312034 ISBN-13: 978-1948312035

Zombie Diaries - Fall Semester Senior Year - ZD5
ISBN-10: 1948312042 ISBN-13: 978-1948312042

Zombie Diaries - Senior Graduation - ZD6
ISBN-10: 1948312050 ISBN-13: 978-1948312059

CONTENTS

ACKNOWLEDGMENTS

I dedicate this novel to my wonderful readers and for all the amazing people I've met and those I haven't. To my family and loved ones, all your support will not be forgotten.

This book was made possible by reviews from readers like you.

Thank you

R.W.K. Clark

PROLOGUE

Mavis Harvey took a long drink of iced tea, then set the glass on the small patio table and lay back in her recliner. The sun was shining down all around her, but she was sitting in a comfortable, shaded spot, simply enjoying the ideal weather. A soft breeze blew around her, and it seemed to make the day even more perfect than it already was. She couldn't have asked for a better day to enjoy time alone.

Ever since she had gotten "sick" the fall before, her family had doted on her to the point of suffocation. She loved them all, but sometimes it was just too much. When she did have a chance to just be alone and breathe, she took it. Now was one of those times, and she couldn't be more thankful. It seemed that the sun was brighter, the air smelled better, and the uncomfortable patio chairs were more comfortable at times like these.

Next, her mind went to her best friend, Kim. Having Kim to talk to and laugh with would have been fun, but the girl's life had been changing quickly. Fortunately, Kim's relationship with her boyfriend was growing fast, and Mavis wanted her to be happy.

Everyone had to grow up, after all; it just seemed like it was happening really fast.

She closed her eyes and moaned lightly with pleasure as a smile curved over her lips. The one person that would have made the day any more wonderful than it was already turning out to be was Matt. If he were with her, she would have to call her surroundings, feelings, and everything else "Heaven." But, Matthew Morgan was in Toledo with his parents visiting a sick aunt, and he wouldn't be back until early evening. Well, she would just have to make do without him. The way things were going, Mavis knew that wouldn't be too difficult; she'd just have to tough it out.

Matt… what an amazing friend and boyfriend! Considering all she had been through since the beginning of her junior year of high school nine months ago, she thought she was doing very well, and Matthew Morgan was likely the primary reason. What an insane year it had been! But now it was over, and summer break loomed out before her, full of promise and possibilities. Then she would begin her Senior year, in the fall. If things continued to look up as they had in the last three weeks, since prom and the insane disaster, or what seemed to be a disaster that took place, she had nothing to worry about.

Mavis let her mind turn fully to all of the details of that night for the first time since it all happened. She thought about getting sick all those months ago. The "illness" that had come upon her out of nowhere had temporarily wiped her out; it also made her crave some of the oddest food she had ever had a yearning for in her entire life: raw meat. Not just raw meat, but bloody raw meat. She had gone from sneaking around eating raw liver to hunting for small animals in the woods near Grandma Cabot's house. But this seemingly innocent symptom of what the doctor labeled as anemia didn't just stop there; it quickly elevated to something much worse, something much more confusing and sinister.

She had eaten her first boyfriend and on the very night of homecoming. It hadn't been something she planned; as a matter of fact, she thought she had taken every precaution to keep from giving him so much as a nibble. Yet before she knew it, it was done, and it was something she lived with every single day.

The emotions that accompanied what she had done were a lot to bear. Mavis became a bit depressed by the act; she determined that she would never date again. She began to change the way she dressed, but even though this was partially due to her changing taste in clothing, the desire to turn boys off from wanting to date her was a major contributing factor. In her mind, the entire Goth way of dressing and acting seemed to suit her new self; what she couldn't understand was why the boys (and sometimes girls) continued to swarm around her like flies.

Regardless of her determination to be done with dating forever, Mavis found herself falling for boyfriend number two right before last Winter Formal. Her best friend, Kim Coleman, had convinced her to attend the ball with Colin Handley. A classmate of hers who had also been very close acquaintances with her first boyfriend, Jeff Deason (whom she had chowed-down on before Homecoming). Mavis had really started to like Colin and even though she had come up with some fairly good solutions that would help her avoid turning him into a full-blown meal.

But alas... she had eaten him too, and just before Winter Formal! The worst thing about that was the fact that it had happened in his home, and she had left the scene for his parents to find like a thief in the night. Just thinking about it made her want to scream sometimes.

Somehow, she had gotten away with these acts legally, at least so far. But the fact that she had done such horrendous things to two boys she liked very much threw her for a loop. What was happening to her? Why was she so seemingly determined to make a meal out of the males in her life? She didn't understand any of it! Mavis began to isolate herself, both emotionally and physically, even from Kim. It seemed that a solution would never be discovered, and answers would never be had when it came to the terrible habit that was developing inside of her.

Mavis did the best she could to avoid boys altogether. Being alone with them was no longer an option, even though she seemed to be a bigger flirt than ever before. Her growing Goth-appeal seemed to be drawing them in from all over. Determined to never repeat the terrible things she had done to Jeff and Colin, Mavis began to keep to herself even more.

CHAPTER 1

The new kid, Matthew Morgan, seemed to appear out of thin air, and he wasn't going to take no for an answer. Oh, cute, smart, understanding Matt… how could she not love him? It helped that she firmly believed he loved her too. It made it all so much easier.

Matt had proven himself in such a way that Mavis had ceased to be able to consider or remember what life had been like without him in it. Not only did he know what was really happening to her and causing the symptoms and behaviors she had been demonstrating, but he also accepted her in spite of it all. Matthew was educating her about her own condition while learning more about it himself, and he was going to amazing lengths to help sate her appetite for all things fresh, raw, and dead without harming others in the heat of the moment.

Yes, she had a failure (and a miserable one, at that) during their little prank at prom. Okay, so it was more than a failure, but Matt helped her to buck up and put it behind her. In the last three weeks, he had also shown her all of the things she had to look forward to, and he helped her to see that she simply had to continue to put one foot in front of the other, even if she really was a zombie.

A rattling to her left yanked Mavis out of her own mind, startling her slightly. She turned to see Feisty, the little dog she had gotten from the humane shelter while on her first date with Colin Handley. He was caught in the middle of one of his favorite toys: a plastic donut-shaped Frisbee that was chewed and mangled. The pup fit right through the hole in the middle, and his fat little tummy always got him stuck tight until Mavis or another family member saw fit to rescue him.

Mavis gave a long, leisurely stretch and smiled at the dog; what a high-strung little fellow he was. She loved Feisty and thought about what life would be like, or how she would have lived with it if she had ever eaten him. That would certainly be one to explain to the parents, neither of whom had any idea what type of bizarre reality their daughter's life was.

Why hadn't she eaten him? Well, she and Matthew had discussed that question in passing about two weeks prior. The one thing they could figure out was that Feisty's smell just didn't appeal to her, and with a little perfume, it didn't. When she lifted him to her nose, she smelled nothing but a dog, and sometimes "wet dog." Even after a bath, his aroma didn't attract her, and she had never been tempted to so much as a nibble on him. For this, Mavis was thankful. To eat the dog might just give her away, and she and Matt both had decided it wasn't time to enlighten poor Jane or Todd Harvey about her condition quite yet.

"Mavis, could you please come inside and help me put the groceries away?"

Jane was standing at the screen to the sliding glass door, smiling out at her lazy daughter and slightly shaking her head. Mavis turned to her and stuck her tongue out playfully. Her mother had always been pretty fun and easy going, and it was easy to be herself around her.

"Ugh!" She replied with an exaggerated groan. "Yesss! I'll be right in."

Jane clucked her tongue and chuckled. "See that you are, Missy!"

Mavis swung her feet from the patio recliner to the ground, snatched up her cell phone and iced tea from the table, and stood. Pausing, she turned to Feisty, who was still trapped in the Frisbee and was attacking it with less-than-fierce growls and paws. She fought the urge to laugh out loud at the confused and frustrated pup.

"Here, dummy," she said as she set her things back down and went to save the little pooch from his situation. "I should take this thing away; you do this to yourself every ten minutes."

But she didn't take the toy away because it was Feisty's favorite. Instead, she freed him and flung the mangled Frisbee across the backyard. Feisty bounded off, Mavis was forgotten. She grabbed her things up once more and headed inside to help her mother.

On the way, her stomach gave a loud, obnoxious growl, signifying that Matt would be over within the hour with snacks to tide her over.

R.W.K. Clark

CHAPTER 2

"I'm surprised Matt isn't here; I expected to see him when I got back."

Jane handed off a dozen eggs to Mavis, who stood at the refrigerator with the door open, putting items away one by one. Taking the eggs, she placed them into the space in the door where they belonged and turned back to her mother for two packages of sandwich meat: salami and bologna.

"He'll be here within the hour, probably," Mavis replied. "I expect to see him, anyway."

"So, how are you two getting along?" Jane asked as she handed sour cream to her daughter. "With as much time as you spend together, one would think you are planning a wedding."

Mavis snorted and rolled her eyes at her mother. "Funny, Mom." She tossed the container onto an empty space in the fridge.

Jane snickered and shoved a bunch of plastic grocery bags into a holder made of checkered fabric that hung from a hook in the pantry. "Just kidding. But you two do seem to have something kind of interesting going on. I have to admit, I certainly am glad that Matt waited to spring his true appearance on us slowly; I'm not sure how I would have stomached all the piercings and eyeliner on such a good-looking young man."

Mavis closed the refrigerator and laughed as she thought about how her Goth boyfriend had wisely dressed the way a normal young man would the first time he met her parents. In the last few weeks, Matthew had slowly, but surely, eased them into his preferred style of dress and appearance. Before anyone even knew what had hit them, Matt looked completely like himself, and no one even batted an eye. It had taken him less than a month, but her mother and grandmother still hassled her about her choice in clothing and pasty white makeup and heavy eyeliner.

Her stomach gave another leap, and Jane guffawed loudly. "Mavis, find something to eat. Why do you wait until you can barely function? Not to mention how disgusting it is to let your stomach growl obscenely around other people."

"I'm waiting for Matt," she shot back. "We're eating lunch together. As a matter of fact, I'm going to go change."

Mavis had been wearing blue jean cut-offs and a black bikini top when lounging in the back. The truth was, she hadn't been planning on eating lunch with Matt, just for him to bring her lunch, but now she had to follow through with her little fib and change clothes. Way to go, Mav.

Darting off to her room, Mavis occupied herself with changing clothes. She thought about Matt while she did, wondering most of all what he would be bringing her for lunch. As she pulled on her shirt, she was overcome with a feeling of gratitude; what would she do without him, especially after she practically cleaned out the entire junior class at prom? If it weren't for Matt taking the upper hand to educate and help care for her apparent need for flesh and blood, Mavis certainly would have unknowingly continued to engage in violent, destructive behavior. Matt's provision, right or wrong, allowed her to continue to be free.

In the distance, Mavis heard the doorbell, and her heart began to pitter-patter. Funny how she got so excited about seeing Matthew each and every time he came over. What she didn't know for sure was if it was because she missed him or because he brought her fresh meat. With a shrug and a final glance in the mirror, she darted out of her room and headed to the door. When she got there, Matt stood in the entryway, smiling.

"Well, looky-look," he greeted her. "And to think that I assumed I would find you lazing around. I should have known better."

Mavis stood on her toes and gave him a kiss on the cheek. Her nearness to him sparked her sense of smell, and she got a big whiff of something bloody, raw, and yummy. Her eyes shifted to a small lunch cooler that was sitting at his feet. Matt immediately took note of her realization and bent down to retrieve the plastic box.

"I brought some leftover cake that my mother wanted you to have." She could tell he was lying by the sparkle in his eyes. "Wanna hang out in your room for a bit?"

Mavis could feel her mother standing within earshot. "What about lunch?"

Matt was on top of things. "I just wanted to tell you about my day. You can have a couple bites of this in the meantime; it's just a small piece."

The two started off down the hall to Mavis' room with her in the rear. She gave a final look back toward the kitchen before closing and locking the door behind them. As she turned to her boyfriend, her stomach gave another obnoxious groan.

Matt held out the cooler. "Here, girl, jeesh! It's just a critter I found in the live trap just this afternoon. But I have some pretty good news for you."

Mavis was already opening the cooler, which held a small raccoon that seemed to be lethargic. Matt had been sort of knocking them out before bringing them, which allowed her to actually kill the animals for herself. Frankly, she could have done without all that killing; she went through thirty black garbage bags a week trying to keep the blood from the floor. All she wanted was the meat, and it was nice when she could focus on that alone. But this was a tiny detail that Matt had yet to get a firm grasp on, let alone Mavis herself.

She grabbed up the animal in both hands and removed it from the cooler. It stirred just a bit, which freaked her out, and she reacted by slamming the creature's head as hard as she could on the floor until it gave a squeal and died. Mavis looked up at Matt and smiled.

"It would be easier if they were dead first," she teased.

Matt shrugged. "Well, sometimes it takes me a bit to get over here with it, and I want it to be warm."

"Good point."

Mavis hopped up and began digging through her closet for a large garbage bag to cover the floor while she ate. It never ceased to amaze her how much of a mess blood could make, and the big bag was what protected her floor, just as it protected her from the wrath she would face with her mother. "Better safe than sorry" was her motto when it came to this.

It took a few short seconds to spread out the garbage bag and dig into the late lunch that Matt had brought for her. While she tore into the small raccoon, Matt flipped through channels on the flat-screen television, stopping at a hard rock music video. With a smile, he settled back onto Mavis' bed and intently watched the television. In about ten minutes, Mavis was wiping her face with baby wipes and folding up the raccoon scraps, bones, and fur safely inside the bag that she had eaten it on.

Continuing on to her hands with a fresh baby wipe, Mavis finally spoke. "So, you mentioned some good news or something like that. What's up?"

Without skipping a beat, Matt grabbed the remote and muted the TV, then turned to her with a smile. "So, I have a new job, and it's one that will do both of us a lot of good."

Mavis shifted her eyes from her hands and gave him

a surprised look. "I didn't know you were even looking for a new job."

Now Matt was literally beaming. "Well, I wanted it to be a surprise if I got it, and I did. So, ask me what the new job is all about."

"What's the new job all about?" she echoed.

Matt puffed out his chest and pretended to adjust a non-existent collar on his t-shirt. "You are looking at one of the new slaughterhouse employees at Miller's Packing House. Cows and pigs galore, and I get to make the killing."

Mavis stared at him, her eyes brightening more and more with each passing second. "You got a job at Miller's Pack? Are you serious?"

Matthew didn't have to spell out for Mavis what a job at the pack meant. For one, everyone in Greenville knew that an entry-level position there paid better than anyplace else, especially for a kid who was just going into their senior year in high school. Secondly, it meant that Matt would be able to easily provide Mavis with ultra-fresh meat, and it would already be dead. As these thoughts rushed around in her mind, Mavis' eyes sparkled as though she were star-struck; she couldn't have been happier.

"Oh, Matt, that's incredible! Now there won't be any more trapping or sneaking around for you and me when it comes to food!" She crawled over to him on her hands and knees, gave her hands a quick glance to make sure there was no blood on them, then wrapped him in a big embrace. "This is really cool!"

Matt hugged her back, his own smile glued to his face. "I know. Right? Best of all, with all the meat I'll have access to, we won't have to worry about you slipping up so much if you know what I mean."

Mavis let go of him and looked him in the eye, concern suddenly filling her expression. "But what if you... you know, get caught for stealing it?"

"Don't worry," he reassured her. "I've been doing some research on slaughter processes in different animals, and I'm pretty sure I have a solid plan." He stroked her hair during a brief pause, then continued. "Besides, I'll be training for the first two weeks, so during that time, and until I have the process down pat. Until I know what I can and can't get away with, well, we have the traps."

Of course, she thought. Matt always paid attention, and he always thought ahead about everything. He wouldn't slip up and risk another disaster like the one at the junior prom. She could trust him to not get himself arrested as well. Slowly, her concern turned into deep trust and sincere peace; Matt would never let her down, and she knew it.

He gazed at her and began to stroke her long black hair once again. "I love you, Mavis Harvey."

"I love you too, Matt," she cooed back. "Now, we'd better leave before my mom starts getting suspicious as to why we're still here."

Matt stood and pulled her to her feet, then picked up the big wad of carcass-containing trash bags and tucked them out the bedroom window to be retrieved for the garbage. Soon, he was tucking the wad into the trunk of his car, and the pair were heading to Sports Burger to get Matt some lunch of his own.

Neither one of them could have been happier.

CHAPTER 3

Detective Ben Gordon of the Greenville Police's Homicide Division unlocked his office door, stepped inside, and immediately hung his suit coat on the coat tree by the door. Giving a long, languishing stretch, he then walked over to the Mr. Java pot and pushed the brew button. Ben Gordon had given up on station house coffee years ago, preferring to brew his own since he was the only one who seemed able to get it right.

While the coffee began brewing, Ben walked over to his desk and plopped down in the black leather chair. He took a deep breath and looked over at the top drawer on the left side of the desk. In the drawer was his work for the day, the same work that he faced every day since the insane murder of Westside High School's star football player Jeff Deason.

The murder of that boy ended up being the tip of the iceberg. While he and his team were trying to narrow down the suspects, another murder happened, just before the high school's Winter Formal. That victim, Colin Handley, had been yet another football player. While it was a gruesome killing, there had been some major differences in the crime scenes left behind.

Yesterday, at his wits' end, Ben had sat down in his locked office in the evening hours, frustrated by the nagging feeling that the recent mass killing at Westside's Junior Prom was somehow connected to the first two. Needing to identify specifics and refresh his mind on the case, Ben had stayed until after one in the morning reviewing the files on the cases, trying to find anything that might take him in the direction of solving not one, but all three cases once and for all.

That was when he seemed to register that both murdered boys had been dating the same girl at the time of their deaths: Mavis Harvey.

Today, Ben Gordon was planning to pay a visit to Mavis and ask her some important questions. First, though, he wanted to find out what he could about her specifically. Was this girl in any way capable of such horrendous acts? Even if she was, she couldn't possibly be capable of wiping out everyone at the dance, could she? The similarities among all three cases, like the eating of flesh, for instance, seemed far too gruesome for a girl of her age.

Ben booted his computer then rose to pour a cup of coffee. As he did, he thought through his strategy. First, he would call Westside High and find out what kind of student, and person, this Mavis was. Then he would look to see if she had any kind of criminal record or any type of police interaction at all. Once he had the goods on her, he would be ready to pay her a visit.

The first thing the detective did when he sat back down he took a healthy chug of his coffee, then he brought up his search engine on the computer and got the number for Westside High. Using the eraser end of a half-dead pencil, he punched the digits into the phone and asked to speak to the principal.

"Hal Pearson speaking." A deep male voice picked up after he was transferred.

Gordon cleared his throat and began to speak, first introducing himself, explaining his business with the educator, and asking a few brief questions about student Mavis Harvey, all while jotting down the man's responses in a pad of paper. He was told that she was one of the best students at Westside, pulling top-notch grades and being a favorite of nearly all of her teachers. Pearson then let the detective know that, since the girl had suffered a couple of different traumas with the loss of two boys she dated, she had changed somewhat. Now she seemed to have gone "Goth," as the man put it, but her grades and attendance remained second-to-none.

When the conversation was over, Ben Gordon proceeded to get on the computer and log into the police system. Once he was in, he went about looking up the girl for legal issues and found that she had never been in any kind of trouble a day in her life. The two things he was able to find was a restraining order and an assault call involving her, and she had been the victim of that. As it turned out, two classmates attacked her and pulled her into an alley to administer a beating. Their efforts were thwarted, both by Mavis and onlookers.

The attackers in the case had been one Shanice Hall,

and a sidekick of hers named Candy Wilkes. According to interviews given by Mavis, they were angry with her for confronting them during a bullying session in the girls' bathroom at Westside. Both of the girls were expelled from Westside as a result of the attack. They were also arrested and charged with assault and battery, slapped with a restraining order by Mavis, and given three months in juvenile detention, which resulted in the girls failing the eleventh grade.

But none of that was what really interested Ben Gordon. What got his attention was the words that Shanice uttered during one of her police interviews. It seemed that the little brat had some kind of fit that nothing was turning out the way she wanted, and that she was actually in trouble for hurting someone. She made a statement in a moment of fury that if police thought she and her friend had hurt Mavis before, they would be shocked when she was all the way done with her. Obviously, nothing had happened overtly; there were no more charges or reports filed. But it was very interesting that she made such a threat in police presence at all.

While they seemed like nothing more than a distraction, Gordon wrote both of their names on his paper. He was going to have a talk with Mavis Harvey, feel her out, and find out what she had to say about the assault incident. Then, just to ease his own mind, he would pay a visit to both Shanice Hall and Candy Wilkes.

It wouldn't be the first time in the history of the

world that a sixteen-year-old girl made good on a threat concerning a high school nemesis, now would it? Far-fetched or not, Ben intended to cover all of his bases. If the pair of hoodlum females had nothing to do with any killings, he would put them out of his mind and move on.

R.W.K. Clark

CHAPTER 4

Mavis plopped down on her beanbag chair in her room, laughing hard at a joke Matt had just told her about three old ladies getting their hair done in a nursing home. She was laughing so hard and loud that she didn't realize her mother was knocking on the door of her room. Matt, who was highly amused by her obnoxious laughter, answered Jane's knock while smiling at Mavis' guffawing form.

"There is a police officer here to see you, Mavis," Jane said as soon as the laughter died down.

Looking up at her mother and seeing the serious, concerned look on her face, Mavis immediately sat upright, terrified. "I'll be out in just a minute."

Jane stepped away from the bedroom door, and Matt closed it softly behind her. Shifting his look to Mavis, he knit his brow. She simply met his gaze, concern of her own written all over her face.

"Why would the police want to talk to you?" Matt asked in a low voice.

Mavis couldn't feel her heart pounding, of course, but if it were still beating at all, it would be pounding. "I can think of one reason. I suppose I had better go find out, though."

She stood up from the bean bag chair and took a deep breath. With Matt behind her, she left the bedroom and made her way out to the family room, where she could see her mother handing a cup of coffee to a man in a suit. Her father was at work; yet right at that moment, Mavis really wished that he was home. Even though she didn't feel any adrenaline, her mind was filled with fear.

"Hi, I'm Mavis Harvey."

The man, who had just taken the cup from Jane, turned to her and offered a half-smile in her direction, but it didn't reach his eyes. He had short brown hair that was longish on top and brown eyes; Mavis guessed him to be in his mid-thirties. The cop also wore a suit instead of a uniform, so she knew right away that he was a detective.

"Mavis, I'm Detective Ben Gordon with Greenville's Homicide Division." Gingerly, the detective took a sip of the hot coffee, then gently set the cup on a coaster on the end table next to his chair. "I need to ask you some questions about the murders that took place last year, and the massacre at Westside a few weeks back."

With a cooperative nod, Mavis sat down on the sofa, and Matt took the spot next to her. "This is my friend, Matt Morgan."

"Matt." Detective Gordon gave the young man a cordial nod before pulling a small notebook out of the inside pocket of his suit coat. "Before we begin, I realize that you have experienced quite a bit of trauma this last school year. I am sorry for the losses that you've had to suffer."

"Thank you."

Out of the corner of her eye, Mavis could see her mother sit down in her rocker, and she felt a bit of discomfort at the woman's presence. They were very close, but what if the truth came out right in front of her? It would break Jane's heart to know what her daughter had become, and what she had done.

Ben gave a glance at each of them, then flipped open his notebook, clicked his pen, and poised it over the paper. "I guess we'll just get started, so you can go on with your day. Now, Mavis: you were dating Jeffrey Deason for a short period before homecoming, is that correct?"

"Yes."

"You were the date he was going to be taking to the dance on the night he was killed?"

Mavis dropped her eyes, partially in genuine sadness at the memory, partially in feigned grief. "That's right. But he never showed! He... he stood me up, or at least, that's what I thought at the time."

"Yes," Detective Gordon confirmed. "That's what all the reports stated that were taken, including the one from your friend... um," he paused and flipped back a couple of pages in the small book. "Kim. Kim Coleman."

Mavis nodded.

"No call from him, and no sign at all that he might

have, um, changed his mind about taking you?"

Mavis shook her head.

Gordon scratched something down, then looked up at her again. "And then, fairly soon after the death of Mr. Deason, you began to see Colin Handley?"

Mavis felt embarrassed. "Yes, but I didn't want to see anyone, Colin was very persistent. Kim and her boyfriend thought it would help me to get over Jeff's passing much faster."

Gordon nodded and continued to watch her closely. "You were to attend the winter dance with Mr. Handley, correct?"

Another nod.

Gordon paused, and Mavis could tell he was searching for the right words for whatever it was he was going to ask her next. "But… Mr. Handley didn't show either?"

She shook her head and began to scrunch up her face as though she was going to cry. Matt reached out and put a hand on her shoulder. Mavis reached up and gave it a pat.

"It was like a nightmare," she replied, her voice catching with emotion for real.

Ben Gordon gave a sympathetic nod. "I'm sure. Now, Mavis, I need to ask you some questions about a confrontation you had with Shanice Hall last year."

"Shanice?"

Out of the blue, Matt handed her a tissue, so Mavis dutifully dabbed at her eyes. The thought passed through her head that he was so smart, she was glad to have him in her corner. After all, even though she had eaten both Jeff and Colin, and even went haywire and wiped out most of the junior class, she hadn't meant to. Never once had she intended to harm anyone. As a matter of fact, all she had wanted to do was figure out how to live with the condition she was in.

Ben Gordon cleared his throat. "Yes, Shanice Hall, as well as her friend Candy Wilkes. According to our records, you were attacked by both of these girls after confronting them for bullying another student in the girls' room at school, correct?"

"Yes."

"Have either of them tried to contact you or communicate with you in any way?" Ben sat forward and concentrated on Mavis' confused face. "I mean, have you ever received any threats from either of them since the incident took place?"

Mavis squinted her eyes to think. "No. I haven't spoken to or even seen, either of them since it happened. Shanice threatened me, you know, just saying she was going to get me, but that was the day it happened. Otherwise, not at all."

Ben began to scribble on his pad once again. "Were those her exact words: 'I'm going to get you'?"

Mavis gave a shrug. "I can't recall specifically. It was something like that, or maybe that she would make me pay, something like that. I didn't pay any attention to her, because she was always full of hot air. Shanice is not a good person, Detective Gordon."

Gordon was jotting furiously now, nodding as he

went. Mavis glanced at her mother, who happened to be looking at her like she was a poor little victim in the entire situation. Mavis felt a pang of guilt and turned her attention back to the cop, who was now taking another drink of his cooled-down coffee.

He put down the cup and sat back in the chair. "So, you didn't attend prom at all, from what I understand."

"No," she replied. "I guess you could say I had enough of dances by then."

"Understandably so." He began to write again, then looked up at Matt. "You didn't try to convince her to go, young man?"

Matt shrugged, and his cheeks reddened shyly through his stark white skin. "Of course. But she was sort of… inconsolable. At least, she was at the time. I'm hoping to convince her this year. I promised I would never stand her up."

Ben Gordon closed his tablet and put it back into his suit coat, then drained his coffee cup and smiled at Jane. "Thank you for the delicious coffee, Mrs. Harvey." He turned back to the kids. "I just want to remind you both that whoever killed those boys, and the junior class, is still out there. We're sure it's the same person. Unfortunately, it's taking more work."

He paused and stood up, popping his pen in his pocket as well. "I will say this," he continued. "I believe the murders all lead back to you, Mavis. Not as a suspect, don't get me wrong. But I am suspicious that whoever committed them did it to get back at you somehow."

Mavis thought about his words. "I could see that with Jeff and Colin, but the entire junior prom?"

Gordon shrugged. "I'm of the belief that the intent there was to find you. You weren't there, and what followed was a result of rage. So, everyone be careful, and Mavis, if you remember anything that might be pertinent, any enemies or anything, please let me know."

Detective Gordon left them, shaking hands all around and leaving his business card for their convenience. Jane watched him as he made his way to his car, as did Matt. Mavis stared down at her hands, her mind racing.

"Can you believe it?" Jane muttered from where she stood at the window. "Someone might have it in for you so terribly as to murder your friends?"

Mavis stood up, her head swimming. "No. No!"

R.W.K. Clark

CHAPTER 5

"So, what you're telling me is that you stood up off the couch and just… spaced-out, just like that?"

Kim Coleman was sitting on the bean bag chair on Mavis' floor, painting her toenails with a greenish-orange color called "Frog Guts" from the Suburbia Rot polish line. Mavis was on the bed, filling her in on the visit from Detective Gordon earlier that day. Her parents were in bed, Matt was busy at his first night on the job at the packing house, and Kim was going to spend the night with her because her own boyfriend, Shawn Maher, was attending a two-day football camp.

"Yes," Mavis replied with a bit of annoyance in her voice, "just like that. It was the creepiest thing ever. I've never spaced-out before in my life. It was like, one minute I was talking, and the next I was staring into the faces of Mom and Matt. Just weird."

Kim paused and looked up at her. "So, what do you think caused it? Nerves over the whole truth of the deal?"

Mavis thought about it for a moment, then shook her head. "No. I didn't get the impression that the detective was on to me at all. As a matter of fact, I think it was because of the memories he invoked with his questions. It seemed to me that he thinks I have some 'enemy' who is doing the murders to get back at me for something."

"Enemy?" Kim scrunched her nose and went back to her toes. "You don't have a single one that I know of."

"Well," she replied slowly. "He seemed to think that Shanice might have something to do with it."

Now Kim stopped with her nails completely, put the brush back into the small jar, and turned her full attention to her best friend. "Why the heck do they think Shanice had anything to do with it? She wasn't even at Westside anymore after she and her sidekick attacked you, so she wasn't around for any of the dances. That's crazy."

Mavis lay back, propping her head and shoulders up with her pillow. "Well, he says something about a threat she could have made or something like that. I guess that I don't remember specifically, but I do know that he had reasons to be suspicious from the way he sounded. He even warned me, Mom, and Matt to be careful. "Whoever" the killer is, they are still out there, and he thinks they have it in for me." She paused thoughtfully, then continued. "The detective thinks it's revenge on me that got both Jeff and Colin killed, and he also thinks that the murders at junior prom, well, the murderer was looking to kill me, but I wasn't there."

Kim shrugged and took the nail polish brush out and started to polish again. "I would think that's a pretty good thing for him to think, all things considered."

"Yeah. I suppose."

The girls were quiet for a bit, then Kim asked, "So, is Matt stopping by tonight?"

Mavis knew that he was; he would be bringing her something fresh to eat and leaving it at the back window. She and Matt had told Kim about her condition after prom, so she knew that Mavis had her little eating habits that were disgusting, but Mavis never indulged her appetites in front of her friend. After all, she had passed out cold when Mavis had bit into a squirrel in front of her at Connor Park, right before prom. Her condition might be something her lifelong friend accepted, but she didn't understand the ins and outs of it, and she certainly wasn't ready to watch Mavis beat a small animal about the head and sink her teeth into it. Maybe once Matt was able to sneak her a liver or heart or tongue from the meat packing plant, she would be able to have her meals in front of her confidante and best friend.

"So, what time will he be here?" Kim asked.

Mavis shrugged and grabbed the remote to the TV. "Hard telling. I know he is getting off at eleven; he is training on the second shift. But his regular summer shift will be nights, so I'm guessing he'll pop by after he's off."

"Won't your mom get pissed?"

With a shake of the head and a smile, Mavis replied, "Naw. My parents really like him. Just like always, they seem to give me more trust than I deserve."

"Are you doing it yet?" Kim paused, nail brush froze in mid-air and a conniving smile on her face.

Mavis stuck out her tongue. "No. But the way I'm feeling, I sure hope it's soon!"

Both girls broke out in hysterical laughter, which incited her father Todd to yell for quiet from her parents' bedroom. Getting control of herself, Mavis began to flip through the TV channels. After a couple of minutes, she settled on a rerun of *The Cravens*, a sitcom that had been a favorite since it had come out. She watched the program while Kim, who was spending the night, moved on to the nails on her other foot and simply listened, laughing in all the right parts.

After the show, Mavis went out and popped popcorn at her friend's request, then returned to the bedroom. The girls were going to watch a movie called *Box Office Butcher*; it was just after ten. Mavis needed to stay awake while she waited on any word from Matt, who would likely knock gently on her bedroom window when he arrived. The best way to pass the time would be by watching television, so their plans for the night were settled.

Though the scary movie was fairly good considering the slashing and all, Mavis found her eyes getting heavy about halfway through. She propped herself up further and even fetched a couple of cold sodas from the refrigerator to give her a little boost, but before she knew it, she was snoring lightly, the movie and her friend left still in the reality which slipped away as she began to dream.

Mavis was leaving Flair Foods, humming to herself as she went. The sun was warm, and she could smell flowers in the air; it was a beautiful day. She was carrying something, and a glance down told her it was her little cooler. By the weight of it, she knew it was packed full of freshly purchased raw liver.

She began to walk home, her cooler swinging gently in her hand as she went. Before she knew it, she was at the big privacy fence right before the alley. A feeling of dread came over her, and she knew exactly who she was going to encounter. This time, though, she wouldn't let anyone, so much as lay a hand on her.

As if on cue, the two of them stepped out of the alley: Candy Wilkes and her "boss," Shanice Hall. They were both smiling, but their teeth were red with blood, and their eyes were nothing but the pupil, black like the night. They both looked like they had been infested with demons, and Mavis knew they meant her harm once again. She stopped and looked at them both, a smile curving over her own lips.

Shanice opened her mouth to speak, and one of her teeth fell out, tumbling down her chin and hitting the ground with a couple of clicks. A shiver ran down Mavis' spine. Oh, yes. They fully intended to try and get the best of her once again.

"You did it," Shanice spat, blood flying from her lips. "You're the one, and we know it. You're a monster, and now you are trying to put the blame on us. It's not going to happen."

Candy laughed, and bloody spittle flew from her mouth as well.

Mavis' smile faded. "You don't know anything."

Candy crossed her arms over her chest and nodded knowingly. "We know more than you think. We know what you eat, and we know that you kill. Maybe we should kill you."

"Off with her head!" Shanice screamed the words, a bloody tooth flying from her mouth along with the words.

Both girls stepped toward her slowly, their arms out in front of them as if they were the zombies. Mavis looked around for someone to help her, and she saw several people, but all of them just stood and stared. Their faces were all the same: stark white masks with nothing but eye holes and horrid smiles. No one moved to help like they did last time. Everyone just watched, frozen in place, anxious to see the outcome of the confrontation taking place before them.

Mavis was terribly afraid…

She took a step back, and the two bloody girls continued to advance. She dropped her cooler without even realizing it and began to shake her head. They were going to beat her to a pulp, and everyone around them was just going to stand there and watch.

"I didn't," she muttered. "I didn't mean to do any of it."

Shanice laughed. "Oh, you meant it. You ate those people, and now you mean to blame us. But we are going to eat you first!"

They continued toward her, and she began to yell for help from anyone that would listen, anyone that would come to her rescue, but no one did. Now, all the people on the street were laughing through their masks, and she heard a couple of them say, "eat her! Eat her before she eats all of us!"

She took two more steps back, and then Shanice and Candy were on her, biting at her flesh and ripping at her with their hands.

Mavis began to scream…

∞

"Mavis, wake up!"

She jerked out of her nightmare instantly to see both Kim and Matt hovering over her, concern all over their faces. Her hands were flailing in the air, and she immediately came to her senses. Sitting up, she gasped for breath; if her heart had a beat, it would have pounded right through her chest.

"Oh, my," she said with relief.

Matt sat down on the bed and took her in his arms, stroking her hair and speaking softly and soothingly to her. "It's okay… it's gonna be fine. It was a bad dream; you're awake now, Mav. It isn't real."

It took her a bit, but she was finally able to calm herself. Unfortunately, the details of the dream didn't fade as her consciousness was gained. Instead, she continued to recall everything in great detail, and it took all of her mental strength to try and shut it out of her mind.

"What was it, Mav?" Kim asked. "What was the

dream about?"

Her face scrunched up, and a single tear trickled down her cheek with the recollection. "It was Shanice and Candy. They were… they were going to eat me, and Greenville was cheering them on."

"It wasn't real, Mavis," Matt reassured.

She nodded and wiped at her eyes. "I know. I'm the one that eats people, not them."

CHAPTER 6

Detective Gordon drove purposefully down his lane on the freeway, a somber look on his face. Since interviewing Mavis, he had set his sights on talking to the two girls who had attacked her in the alley the previous fall. As it turned out, both of their families had relocated to accommodate the fact that the girls had been expelled from Westside High. The trouble was that, so far, he had just been able to locate Candy Wilkes and her family. They had moved to Toledo.

He had yet to track down Shanice Hall, and that concerned him just a bit.

Now the detective was on his way to the Wilkes residence. He called and spoke with Candy's mother, who agreed to let him talk to her. He hadn't let on that he was motivated to interview the girl by suspicion; Gordon had simply told the woman that Candy might unknowingly have information regarding the two dead football players from the previous year. Though her mother told him she had no idea how she could, Gordon convinced her that he had to cover all his bases.

As for Shanice, well, his research thus far had turned

up nothing as to her location. She wasn't enrolled in any local school, and the principal at Westside told him that they had forwarded her records to Reagan High in Cleveland. But when Ben contacted that school, he was told that she had been removed by her parents to be home-schooled right after winter break. He was able to turn up no address or telephone number for any of the Hall family; he hoped that she and Candy had remained in contact and that she would be able to fill in the blanks as to her whereabouts for him.

Ben Gordon took the next exit off the freeway. According to his smart phone's GPS, he would arrive at the Wilkes residence in approximately ten minutes. With his right hand, he felt around on the passenger seat until he found his files. If he didn't have the files, he would be thinking about missing something during the entire interview, and that wouldn't be conducive to quality detecting.

Ben followed the GPS's verbal cues on autopilot, not even paying attention to his surroundings. Next to him on the passenger seat sat a file folder with the name "Candy Wilkes" on the tab in black permanent marker; it was that folder that his mind was on. He had the months-old mug shot of the girl memorized from her arrest for the assault on Mavis. He was picturing that photo, preparing himself for the meeting.

Before he knew it, Ben was in front of a quaint split-level home with immaculate landscaping, which was guarded by a couple of gnomes that appeared to be fighting over a garden hose. On closer inspection, he realized that while they appeared to be fighting, they were really no more than a very clever hose holder, and the realization brought a smile to his face; his wife would have gotten a kick out of it.

Grabbing up the folder, Ben popped a mint into his mouth, shut off the ignition, and headed up the walk to the front door. He walked up the long sidewalk, his skills of observation in overdrive, taking in every last detail around him. Doing this was second nature to him, something he constantly did when awake, even at home. Ben never even gave it a second thought, but when he was a beat cop, the skill had saved his life on more than one occasion.

There was a small concrete porch with iron railings on either side; merely three steps to take to get to the door. Whoever was in charge of the Wilkes home today had the screen door closed, but the inner door was wide open. Through it, Ben could see a woman in her mid-thirties crocheting and glancing up at a television show periodically. He didn't see a teenaged girl anywhere, but he stood and watched in silence for a brief moment, taking things in, before ringing the doorbell and gaining the attention of the female inside.

"Detective Gordon?" The woman had put down her crocheting and rushed to the door. Now she was holding open the screen and inviting him inside.

Ben thanked her with a smile and a nod while she rushed to the remote control and turned off the television. Turning around and returning his smile, she then gazed in the direction of a hallway off to his left.

Gordon braced himself, sure she was going to yell for Candy at the top of her lungs. Instead, she paused and motioned for him to have a seat, then hollered for the girl.

Gordon sat on one end of a loveseat and placed the file folder next to him. The woman turned back to him and asked if she could get him something cold to drink. He agreed and watched her as she disappeared into the kitchen. Ben Gordon stifled a chuckle; her sweet, soft voice sounded nothing like the scream she had emitted moments before.

While the woman was out of the room, Candy Wilkes entered.

She came up the hallway slowly, hands clasped in front of her, arms straight down. Ben Gordon automatically stood and offered a stiff smile, knowing that it was her, but a bit taken back by her appearance. She looked nothing like her mugshot picture from the year before… nothing at all.

In the mugshot, Candy's hair had been short, in a style that was mussed and spiky, and it had been died a bright red, almost orange. Now, months later, her hair was a light brown, shoulder length, and pulled back from her face on both sides in a conservative fashion, wisps of bangs falling over her forehead.

Also, in the picture, she had been wearing a tank top which had shown a lot of cleavage, more than a sixteen-year-old should ever be showing. Today, Candy was wearing a denim skirt that fell below the knee, and she had it paired with a conservative short-sleeved, plain white t-shirt top which was long enough to cover the top of the skirt by three to four inches, no belly buttons showing today.

Her face was devoid of makeup, making her look to be about fourteen, though Gordon knew that she was now seventeen. At the time she was arrested for helping to assault Mavis Harvey, her makeup had been so heavy, with much caked around her eyes and on her lips. It had been smeared around due to the physical confrontation, giving her a hard, harsh look. Today, the girl standing before him had a much softer effect, contrasting everything he was prepared to encounter. The girl was as different from her mugshot as white was to black.

Detective Gordon held out his hand, still a tad bit unsure that this was the same girl he wanted to talk to.

"Candy Wilkes?" he asked, hand in mid-air.

The girl glanced down at his hand, then stepped forward and offered her own. "Yes."

"Candy… please sit."

The two shook, then they both sat down, Ben on the loveseat and Candy on the matching sofa. Her mother reappeared with a tray carrying three glasses of iced tea. She gave one to Ben first, then held the tray down to her daughter before taking the last one for herself. The woman placed the empty tray on the empty end of the sofa, then sat down in the chair she had been occupying when he had arrived.

"Well, Candy, I must say that your appearance has changed drastically from last year, and for the better." He took a sip of his tea. "I could hardly recognize you from the picture we took at the station."

Mrs. Wilkes didn't give Candy a chance to respond. "You know, Detective, the outer appearance tells others a lot about the state of the inner person. Candy has made many changes, and the way she looks now reflects those changes clearly."

Ben smiled slightly, not missing the standoffish tone the woman had in her voice. "Well, it suits you, Candy."

"Thank you," the girl muttered, her face bare of all emotion.

"Well, I suppose we should get started."

He put his tea on an available coaster sitting on an end table right next to him. Grabbing up his file folder, he set it on his lap and opened the cover; the photo of her was on top. Giving it, and Candy, one more comparable glance, Ben flipped the photo over onto its face and turned his attention to the next page, the original police report concerning the assault.

"So, Candy, I just need to ask you a few questions about the assault on Mavis Harvey and some other incidents that took place after that." Gordon picked up the report and squinted at it, then looked over the top of the page at the girl, who appeared to be bored already. "Are you ready?"

She nodded.

"Now, your honesty is imperative." He set the paper back on top of the stack in the folder. "Why, Candy, did you and your friend Shanice decide to jump Mavis in the alley last year?"

The girl offered up something of a partial shrug,

glanced at her mother, who was glaring at her a bit, and replied, "Shanice was angry because she got her into trouble over some girl she was pushing around in the school bathroom."

"Donna Reilly, correct?" Ben had pulled out his trusty notebook and had his pen poised over the paper; Candy gave him another nod. "So, what was that about? Why was Shanice bothering her?"

Candy knit her brow and stared at something invisible on the floor. "No particular reason. That's just how Shanice is… or was, anyway."

"What do you mean, 'was'?" Candy's choice of past-tense wording caught his attention immediately. Was Shanice alive and well somewhere, or was she, too, the victim of someone's violent temper?

Another shrug. "I haven't seen her or talked to her since. We're not friends at all anymore; I guess that's the reason I said was."

Ben Gordon gave an understanding nod but made a note anyway. He knew from his years of experience that every little thing added up, and there was nothing that meant nothing at all. People were intelligent, but no one was that smart.

"So, the reason for the assault on Miss Harvey was simply because she stood up to Shanice?"

Candy snorted, and her mother picked up a paperback romance novel and threw it at her out of disapproval. The book hit her on the arm and fell to the sofa; Candy's hand went to the spot on her arm and rubbed it as if the featherlight book was going to leave a bruise. Ben was amused by the action; the girl seemed to take the victim-stance in every situation, and that was something to pay attention to.

"No," Candy finally replied. "The reason for the assault was because Shanice got suspended from school, and she blamed Mavis for it. If Mavis had just minded her own business, none of this would have happened. She should have just left the bathroom and went on her way, but no!"

"Candy!" Mrs. Wilkes was red in the face; the tone that came out of the girl's mouth obviously embarrassed and infuriated her.

Now it was Ben's turn to snort, which he did as he wrote in his tablet. It was just like a bully to blame everyone but themselves for their problems. Candy was no different; her little attitudes were sneaking out here and there, and not all the long skirts and lack of makeup could distract from them.

He sat back and looked at her for a long moment. "Now I want to ask you about the threats made toward Mavis during the booking process you both went through. Did Shanice alone make the threats to 'get Mavis,' or did you make them as well?"

"Oh, it wasn't just her; I definitely made them, because I was being arrested and I was mad. I mean, I was angry!" Candy shot her mother a look, then put her eyes back on Ben. "I mean, at first, I really didn't think we would do anything, but we did, and now it's done."

He studied her carefully. "Did you ever follow through on the threats you made alone?"

"No," Candy said a bit forcefully. "My mother barely lets me out of the house, and after a while, I suppose that I just sort of let it go. She ain't worth it, anyhow."

After a brief pause, Ben asked, "What about Shanice? Did she follow through?"

With a shrug, the girl replied, "I don't know. Like I said, I haven't seen her. Last I knew she moved away."

"Where is she living now, Candy? It seems like she just fell off the face of the earth."

Candy looked over at her mother, who was still giving her the evil eye. "Like I said. I haven't talked to her, so how should I know?"

Ben Gordon knew immediately that the girl was lying through her teeth, and it was likely because her mother had forbidden her to have contact with Shanice, but she had been doing it anyway.

"You know, if you are lying, you are hindering an investigation, don't you? That's a criminal act, and you can be charged with it."

Mrs. Wilkes interrupted. "Listen, this assault case has been resolved, so what is this really all about? My daughter was arrested and did the time she was required to do. I have a feeling there is more to this than you are saying."

Ben turned to the woman. "This is about two of Mavis Harvey's boyfriends being murdered within months of each other, and it was done after threats made by these two girls during the arrest process. It also concerns the murders that took place at junior prom, which initially led to Mavis, but as it turned out, she had an airtight alibi and never even attended the dance. We believe that someone, or a couple of people, carried out these acts with both the intention to hurt the girl emotionally and to get her into trouble for the crimes committed at the school."

The woman, who was now getting a much clearer picture regarding Ben Gordon's visit, narrowed her eyes at him. "So, basically, you are suspicious that my daughter had something to do with these incidents? I mean, I agree that it appears that someone has it out for this girl, but haven't you checked out any of her other enemies?"

"Mrs. Wilkes, Mavis Harvey has no other enemies," he told her in a low voice. "As a matter of fact, it seems that she is well liked by everyone at Westside, including her instructors. The one and only confrontation of her life involved Shanice and your daughter, and the murders of the boys began right after this took place." He turned back to Candy. "So, did you have anything to do with these things, or do you know something about who did?"

Candy's attitude really came out now. "I'll just say that, no, I didn't. If Shanice were involved, I wouldn't know anything about it, and even if I did, I wouldn't tell you."

"Candy!" Her mother was getting red in the face. "The detective here is talking about the death of several people! If you know anything, you need to tell him… now."

The girl shot her mother a nasty look, which resulted in a ballpoint pen being thrown at her by Mrs. Wilkes. Candy looked back at Ben, her eyes so narrowed that they might as well not have been open. She was not going to be as cooperative as he had hoped. The truth was; he was thoroughly convinced that even if she wasn't directly involved, she knew much more than she was telling him.

Ben shook his head in frustration. "I doubt very highly that your best friend wouldn't have mentioned it to you if she did something like that. Let's consider the fact that you were the one who assisted her in the initial assault. You were the one who bullied other kids with her continually. You are the one the evidence has led me to talk to right now."

"Like I said, Detective Gordon, I don't know anything, but I certainly feel like she's gotten what she deserves." The look on Candy's face turned smug and sarcastic.

Shocked with her words, Gordon smiled at her, a knowing smile, one that said, "I know you're lying… I'm onto you."

"Are we finished now?" Candy was sneering.

Mrs. Wilkes answered for Ben. "You are. As a matter of fact, go to your room; I'll deal with you in a bit."

The girl stood up and sulked off, saying nothing to Ben or her mother, but stopped in the hall from which she had come, listening. Ben began to put his file folder back in order while Mrs. Wilkes stood up. She waited patiently for him to get organized and rise to his feet as well.

"Detective Gordon, I'm sorry for my daughter's attitude; I just don't understand why she would want to cover for such a mean girl as Shanice Hall." The look on the woman's face told him she was stricken with concern as if she believed that maybe her daughter knew much more than she was telling. She turned to the girl, and in a much gentler voice said, "Candy, if you know something that will take a killer off the streets, you need to help the detective by sharing the information you do know."

But Candy wasn't going to bend, and he knew it. He held up his hand as a way of silently telling Doris Wilkes that it was okay, that teens couldn't be explained, particularly when they were facing trouble, or at least were privy to it.

"One last question, ma'am," he said, smiling. "You wouldn't happen to have any idea where the Hall family is living now, do you?"

Mrs. Wilkes shook her head. "Last I knew they moved to Cleveland shortly after she got out of detention for the assault. But I can poke around and ask some of the women in my book club; her mother had belonged as well. Maybe one of them has maintained contact. If I find out anything, I'll be sure to let you know."

Ben Gordon handed her one of his business cards, shook her hand, and thanked her for her time. As he walked down the sidewalk to his car, he thought about

Candy Wilkes. He thought about the drastic change in her appearance, her strict home-schooling mother, and the vast differences in her life since the assault had taken place. She might have looked milder, but she was certainly one angry girl, and anger could drive people to do some pretty crazy things.

R.W.K. Clark

CHAPTER 7

Mavis and Jane sat at the kitchen table the following morning. Jane drank coffee while Mavis shoveled in bacon, eggs, and hash browns. She no longer had any kind of appetite for regular food; she simply ate it to appease her mother and father, both of whom were still completely oblivious to her zombie state.

Jane was chatting to her about Grandma Cabot's garden, and how the family would be helping with yard work on Sunday during their regular dinner with the woman. Mavis was listening to her, partially; her mind was on Matt and what he would be bringing her to eat that day. She was in serious need of some "real" food. It just couldn't be helped, though. No matter how full she managed to make her belly, it was never full enough.

Suddenly, Mavis' cell phone chimed, letting her know she had a text. She glanced at the screen to see that Kim Coleman wanted her to call as soon as she was able. Mavis continued to eat her breakfast and chat with her mother, planning to call Kim after she helped clean up the kitchen. She didn't speak to her friend as often as they used to, so she should have been more excited, but she also knew that Kim was busy with her own love and life.

While she and Jane did the dishes together, the conversation turned to Detective Gordon's visit. Jane was curious about the questions he asked regarding the incident with Shanice Hall and Candy Wilkes. It seemed she was simply blown away by the thought that a young girl might be capable of horrible violence with revenge in mind.

"I know you weren't good friends with either girl," Jane began, "but do you really think that they could do such things? I mean, wouldn't the killer have to be strong to overcome a couple of football players, much less the entire Junior Prom? It just doesn't make any sense to me."

Mavis shrugged as she dried off a plate. "I don't know, Mom. I mean, does murder ever make sense? As for whether or not Candy could or would do it, well, I would hope not. I mean, even as angry as she and Shanice supposedly were for getting in legal trouble, it's pretty extreme to murder people just to get back at me. Why the entire Junior Prom? It just doesn't make sense to me, either. If one or both of them did do it, the one thing that might make sense is that they were sick killers, to begin with."

Mavis thought about how easily the lies seemed to come off her tongue lately. The fact that she felt no guilt whatsoever, at least for the time being, about keeping herself out of the suspect limelight surprised her as well. She had always cared about other people, but she had a lot to lose. Not only would she wind up in prison for her deeds, but those same deeds would devastate her family, and that alone was enough for her to continue her charade.

But something did nag at her a bit, and it wasn't guilt for the murders. It was the thought that someone that wasn't responsible would be blamed for them if she was not. In the back of her mind, she wondered what kind of person she really was to let this happen. It hurt her to think that she was so low as to allow something like that to take place just so she could be happy. After a moment, she couldn't take the thoughts, so she pushed them out of her mind with all she had inside of her and focused on the task at hand.

When at last the dishes were done, Mavis snatched up her phone and took Feisty out into the backyard for a potty break. While the little dog pranced around and fought with sticks, she called Kim. The need to talk about everything was weighing heavy on her heart anyway, and Kim knew the truth about her so she could be trusted.

The girl answered the phone on the first ring. "I thought you'd never call. What's going on, anyway?"

"What do you mean?" Mavis asked.

She could hear Kim groan. "Shawn and I went to Flair's this morning to pick up a dozen eggs and orange juice for my mom. I ran into Candy Wilkes; have you seen her lately? She looks like she belongs on 'Little House on the Prairie'! Not to mention the fact that she's weirder than ever; she has this evil way about her like she's kind of losing it."

"Nope. Haven't seen her since last year." Mavis tried to picture the one-time Westside "A-Lister" looking like Laura Ingalls, but she couldn't muster a visual in her mind. "Obviously you talked to her? You think she's kind of losing it, huh?"

"Well, she came up to me, but yeah. She said some cop came to her house asking her questions about the assault, and he wanted to know if she knew where Shanice was living." Kim paused, and Mavis could hear her friend's boyfriend, Shawn Maher, mumbling something in the background, which she answered before continuing. "Anyway, she said the cop sounded like he thinks that she and Shanice have some kind of knowledge about Jeff and Colin, and maybe even the prom deal."

Mavis' stomach did a flip from a tinge of guilt. "Yeah."

She plopped down into one of the patio chairs and sighed. "Well, basically he just verified my version of events, then asked me some questions about enemies, which the only ones I have ever had are Shanice and Candy. He really didn't go into much detail, but from what I could piece together it sounded like he is suspicious of them."

"Wow," Kim replied simply, then said, "Yeah, Candy has a real attitude. I even suggested that maybe they did do it, and all she did was give me this sarcastic kind of laugh, then her mom drug her off. It was like she wanted to brag on it, and we both know she didn't do it. Weird. If that's the way she acted with the cop, it's no wonder that he's warm on her as the killer, you know?"

"That is weird." Mavis gave a shout for Feisty to get out of her mother's flower bed, and the dog obeyed. "Maybe she knows something about the truth somehow, and that's why she laughed." The thought almost made Mavis shudder. For the first time, Mavis considered the fact that someone might have the goods on her. Oh, that would be a disaster! What if someone like Candy really did know, and they were going to use it against her for revenge?

"No," Kim replied. "It wasn't like that. Besides, if she had tried to hint around to the cop that it was you, he would have been back to see you by now, don't you think?"

"Yeah, I guess. I mean, maybe. Heck, Kim, I don't know. I don't know anything anymore, it seems."

Kim continued. "Mavis, don't worry about it. I think she is kind of getting off on the thought that someone thinks she could be capable of such a thing. Anyway, from what I gathered during the brief conversation, it sounded to me like this detective is really bent on tracking down Shanice. I think I'm gonna try an online search for her family."

"You could, I guess," Mavis said. "But I think the cop has likely tried that, and it's gotten him nowhere."

"You're probably right. Besides, he has resources we don't even know about, I'll bet."

Mavis didn't want to talk about it anymore; the subject was making her stomach turn, so she changed it.

The conversation turned to plans Kim and Shawn had for the weekend to go see a new movie and have supper at an Asian restaurant that had just opened up. She tossed an invitation at Mavis, telling her to bring Matt, and she accepted. It would be good to get out of the house with friends and get her mind off all of her stress. Soon after that, the call ended.

Mavis got Feisty's mini tennis ball from his toy basket on the patio and played a bit of fetch with him, trying to cheer up and ignore the guilt she felt, but no matter how hard she tried, it seemed to stay in the back of her mind, tugging and pulling like crazy.

She tossed the ball and thought, Mavis, how could you? How could you let someone take the fall for things that you did, even if they did want to? The voice in her right ear was trying its hardest to make her feel guilty and ashamed.

The voice in her left ear argued with the other one vehemently. No, it said. It wasn't murder at all, none of the times. Murder is when you plan it when you want people to die. It's not something that happens by accident, like with you. You didn't murder anyone.

Feisty brought back the ball, and Mavis threw it again before sitting down on the patio chair, confused and upset. What was she going to do? How was she going to talk to the cops or anyone else for that matter, and lie to them every single time? Sure, it seemed to come easy to her, the lying. Sure, she knew she didn't mean to hurt anyone. She could comprehend that technically speaking, it wasn't her fault that she had eaten two of her boyfriends and most of the junior class. But that didn't change the way she felt inside about everything going on in her life right at that moment.

CHAPTER 8

Ben Gordon sat at his desk, his hands folded together and resting on his chest as he stared blankly at the computer screen. He was sitting back in his chair, frustrated at the lack of information he could find on the family of Shanice Hall, or the girl herself. It was as if the Halls had fallen off the face of the planet.

It was late, nearly eight at night, and the station house was fairly quiet except for an occasional booming laugh or ringing phone from outside the door. The night was fairly dead crime-wise, which really wasn't that unusual for Greenville. Sure, there were crimes, but they were typically minor. The murders of the two Westside football players and the prom massacre were the biggest things to happen there in its history, and it was that group of crimes that kept Ben at the office.

For the last several hours he had been focusing his energies on tracking down Shanice Hall. They had moved to Cleveland after the girl served her time in Juvie, but from there the family just disappeared. After speaking with Candy Wilkes and her mother, he had spoken to several of the Halls' former neighbors. By all accounts, the mother and father were appalled and embarrassed by their daughter's actions, which prompted the move to Cleveland, as well as Shanice's enrollment in a boarding school to the north. Gordon had contacted the school and found out that Shanice had attended a few months before the family moved again. They left no forwarding address, and there had been no request for her school records from any other educator anywhere.

They simply fell off the radar completely.

As for the "all-knowing" Internet, the one thing it could do was confirm all he had learned so far and nothing more. He simply didn't know what to do next. His heart was telling him that the murders of the boys and those that took place the night of junior prom definitely had something to do with the two bully girls, and he had himself convinced that Shanice had been the mastermind of it all. Why else would her family disappear the way they had, without leaving any trace or trail of their whereabouts or existence? They were covering up something, all right, and he was sure that Candace Wilkes was fully privy to the information he was seeking. She was probably involved up to her eyeballs, and the reason that her family hadn't run for the hills was that her parents were oblivious to the truth.

But was Candy really bright enough to cover her rear-end? Ben Gordon believed she was, and he also thought that luck played a part as well. Not to mention she had probably learned some tricks from the devious and conniving Shanice. Regardless, he was going to keep looking for the Halls, that much was certain. But he would also be paying many more visits to Candy. If she was involved on any level, or if she had even the slightest bit of information, he was going to get it out of her.

Greenville was a wonderful place to live. It was clean, quiet, and wholesome, even by the standards of the current age. The fact that so many people had died at the hands of some sick, unknown assailant infuriated him beyond words; he wouldn't rest until he had the culprit in hand. The good news was that Ben was sure he knew exactly who had committed the crimes, and he was angry that so much death had taken place for no other reason than revenge.

Next, he considered the trauma that the murders had on the citizens of Greenville. Not one single person had been left unaffected by all the deaths. It was a small area, and everyone knew everyone else, even though it was technically part of Toledo. That didn't matter; Toledo took an emotional hit because of all of it too. It was a mess, but he was just the person to clean up this mess.

His mind turned to Mavis Harvey. If all of this was truly due to the alley assault the previous fall, then that girl had a bad junior year. For a brief second his mind flirted with the idea that perhaps she had something to do with the murders. After all, she looked like she belonged in a punk rock video; what if she was a Satanist or something? What if her look-alike boyfriend had been in on it too, and the deaths of the Deason boy and the Handley boy had been sacrificial? Was it possible that they had known each other before he transferred to Westside? Was it possible that they were the masterminds behind all of it?

No. There was no way. Appearances aside, all accounts of both Matt and Mavis were top-notch. They were well-behaved students trusted by their families and peers to the extreme. They were respectful, responsible, and had their eyes on the future. The fact that the assault had taken place right before the murders began merely bolstered his belief in Mavis' innocence. Not to mention that Matthew Morgan hadn't even moved to Greenville until spring after Deason and Handley were killed. No, Mavis was innocent in this thing. She might have been the motivating factor, but that did not make her a murderer. Ben was willing to lay money on Hall and Wilkes being the major players in the game, and he would keep following that lead until it became blatantly obvious that he was wrong.

Leaning forward, Ben Gordon began to type, searching for family members of the Halls, either the mother or the father, it didn't matter which. It was time to start digging deeper. He entered the father's name for the hundredth time that day. He was able to come up with enough information to discover that the man had been an only child, and both of his parents were deceased. There were no uncles, aunts, or cousins to be found.

As for Mrs. Hall, it turned out she had been born out of the country, in Ukraine, as a matter of fact. Now, there was a lead! Had the Hall family gone there to start over after their stuck-up teenage daughter had shamed them nearly to death?

He thought so, and now it was time to broaden his search. It was time to look into the lives of Michael and Aneta a bit deeper. Not the lives they were currently living, wherever they were, but the lives they had while they were here. Who worked for Michael in his office? What did they know about the family or even the extended family? Had Michael or Aneta ever mentioned leaving, even in passing? What about Aneta? Who were the friends in her social circle? What did she do in her spare time? What had she told those she considered close to her?

Suddenly, Ben realized he had been asking himself the wrong questions. He needed to be looking deeper into the lives they led while in Greenville, and it was there that he would begin to find the answers he was looking for.

R.W.K. Clark

CHAPTER 9

"Oh, my, Mavis! That movie was so good, wasn't it?"

Kim, Mavis, and the guys were just leaving the movie theater after seeing the show that Kim had been so bent on seeing. It had been something of a romantic "chick flick," which really didn't appeal to Mavis like it would have a year ago, but it had been good enough in its own way. She made an agreeable sound and smiled at her friend to appease her.

Matt and Shawn both had their own opinions.

"Um, I thought it, well, kinda… boring!" Matt was teasing, and Shawn gave a snort for an agreement, prompting Kim to stick her tongue out at them. "I think we should have seen *Dead on the Water*, but no…"

Kim groaned. "Ugh. Who wants to see something like that? Oh, yeah, boys, that's who."

Mavis was ready to change the subject. "So, what's this new Chinese place called again?"

"Chinese Chang's," Kim replied. "From what my dad says, they have the most awesome egg rolls he's ever had in his life. I'm excited. I just love egg rolls."

Mavis nodded in agreement as they piled into her

little car, with Matt in the driver's seat. But the last thing on her mind was egg rolls. Before she and Matt had left to pick up Kim and Shawn, he had brought her a couple of kidneys from his job that he had packed on ice. She had put off eating them so she wouldn't mess up her clothes, but now she was practically beside herself with a hunger for flesh, and she was beginning to smell her friends; they smelled like raw steaks. As Matt pulled out of the theater parking lot, Mavis dug her vapor rub out of her purse and smeared it liberally under her nose. Matt took notice and gave her a wink.

Less than five minutes later, the foursome pulled into the lot of Chinese Chang's and found a solitary parking spot far away from the door. The place was packed, and as far as Mavis could see, there were no empty spots left. Kim was beaming with pride.

"Told you this place is good," she said. "Not only is it a buffet, but my dad also says they have a special-order menu. You can have steaks and everything."

That was all Mavis needed to hear to brighten her mood. "I think I'm going for a super-rare steak, Matt. But don't worry, I'll pay for my own."

"No, babe," he replied as he draped his arm over her shoulders. "I've got you."

They reached the main door and were greeted by a group of laughing diners who were leaving. Upon entry, the four realized that they would be waiting a bit for a table, so they sat at the end of a wood bench in the foyer area and waited to reach the hostess stand. Another group left, and right after that, three people entered and got in line behind them. Mavis' mouth dropped open upon recognizing the newcomers, and she turned to Matt nervously.

"It's Candy Wilkes and her parents!" Mavis' eyes were wide with worry.

He glanced over her shoulder at the trio, then looked back at her. "Just ignore them for now. Soon enough we'll be seated; just keep yourself turned to me."

Mavis gave him a nod and tried to act nonchalant, grateful when Kim, who noticed the Wilkeses as well, began to crack off-the-cuff jokes to help distract her. She would laugh at all the right times but was mostly focused on the rapidly moving line, praying under her breath that they would get a table soon.

Suddenly, Mavis felt a hand on her shoulder; she turned to see Candy staring at her, a cocky smile on her face. The girl's mother and father were chatting, paying no attention to their daughter. Mavis' friends, on the other hand, went immediately quiet.

"So," the girl began, "I got a visit from a cop recently. Did you?"

Mavis cleared her throat and squared off her shoulders; she wasn't about to let the girl see that she was nervous. "As a matter of fact, I did. Sounded to me like he thinks you know something about Jeff, Colin, and the entire junior class for that matter." She turned to face the girl entirely. "So, do you?"

Candy smirked. "Whether I do or don't has nothing to do with you. After the trouble you got me into, I feel like you've had your just desserts. You know, my best friend had to move away because of you. I don't feel a bit sorry about your broken heart. Besides, you're a freak anyway."

Mavis looked the girl up and down. She was wearing conservative black slacks and a pink satin button down with a high ruffled collar; it was buttoned all the way up her neck. Mavis wanted to laugh. Dressed like she was, and without all that makeup she used to wear, both of them could pass for freaks together.

"You're one to talk," she replied.

Suddenly, a pretty, petite Asian girl interrupted. "Excuse, please? How many for a table?"

Matt took Mavis protectively by the upper arm. "Four, please."

"Please follow," the girl said.

Matt turned to Candy and sneered at her, then the four teens followed the girl to the table that was prepared for them. During the short stroll, Mavis shot sideways glances over her shoulder several times at Candy; every time, the girl was glaring at her with a half-smile on her face. Funny, but the way a person dressed or looked could never hide their heart.

The first thing she realized as they settled at their table was the fact that a busboy was cleaning the table right next to them. It was a table for four, but a good look around the place told Mavis that it was soon to be the last available table in the place, and the Wilkes family was next in line. Ugh, she thought as she buried her nose in her menu; Matt had to order water and diet soda for her, she was so distracted.

The girl who seated them soon came back with their drinks. As she passed them out, the Wilkeses were taking their seats at the table next to Mavis and her friends, causing her to groan inwardly once again. The next thing she knew, she could clearly hear Mrs. Wilkes speaking much too loudly to the young man who was seating them.

"There isn't another free table? This really isn't a good spot for us."

The kid turned and gave a glance around the dining room as if he needed to. "No, no other seats."

Mrs. Wilkes rolled her eyes. "Fine, this will do. Three buffets and three iced teas, please."

The young man nodded and left to retrieve the drinks for the Wilkes family, telling them that the plates were at the buffet for their use. Mavis kept her eyes off their table, but she saw Matt was shooting glares while Kim made blatant faces at Candy Wilkes. Poor Shawn, on the other hand, was holding his left hand up to his face in an obvious attempt to pretend he wasn't even there. Mavis groaned.

"Would you all want the buffet or menu?"

The sweet girl who had brought their drinks now looked at them expectantly, waiting to find out what they intended to have. Kim, never one to pass up as much food as she could get, took the helm without hesitation. Mavis wasn't at all surprised; even with her pretty face and curvy figure, Kim Coleman was in no way ashamed when it came to food.

"Three buffets, please," she said with a syrupy tone. "But my friend will order off the menu."

In seconds, Matt, Kim, and Shawn had disappeared from sight. Mavis looked up at the server nervously; the girl simply smiled back sweetly, pen in hand, waiting to take her order. She didn't hesitate, for the sake of awkwardness.

"I'd like a T-bone, rare, with baked potato and corn, please."

The girl scribbled, then paused. "Rare?"

Mavis nodded. "Yes, as rare as humanly possible."

"Humanly?"

Mavis did a mental head slap. "Really rare, please."

The girl tried to maintain a pleasant expression, but Mavis could see the strange look in her eye. Big deal; just bring me the steak, she thought. But she continued to smile pleasantly and nod slightly until the server nodded back once and walked away.

Having forgotten that the Wilkeses were to be their dinner mates, Mavis picked up her water and began to look around as she took a sip. There, directly to her right, was Candy Wilkes. She had a pile of what appeared to be Sesame Chicken on her plate, along with a plate of about five egg rolls. Two small plastic containers of sweet and sour sauce were on the egg roll plate as well. When Mavis was done looking over the food, her eyes met Candy's; the girl spoke immediately.

"You know, my life is so bad because of you that I would gladly stand by and watch you suffer. I'll never feel bad for you, and I'm glad those kids died."

With that, the girl turned her attention fully to her food and began to eat. As if nothing ever happened, she smiled fully at her parents when they returned to the table, and for the rest of the meal, the two didn't look at each other again.

Mavis ate her food in silence when it came, trying to laugh at her friends' jokes in all the right places, but her heart was never really in the laughter. Matt gave her several looks. He knew something was wrong, that something had happened while he caroused the buffet.

While the friends had dinner, Mavis didn't say a single word about Candy Wilkes to anyone. It would do no good, just harm. Matt had a pretty strong tendency to get protective of her, and sometimes he didn't really think about the place or the time. He knew about the assault, and now he knew about the suspicions surrounding the deaths and how Candy was supposedly involved. He was liable to blow a gasket. She would let it drop, and hopefully, they could all enjoy their meals, including the Wilkeses.

By the time the fortune cookies came, the Wilkes family was gone; they didn't even wait for their own cookies. On their way out of the restaurant, Candy brushed hard against her chair, but Mavis ignored the intimidating gesture. That isn't to say that Kim didn't notice, but she said nothing, just looked at her friend protectively and glanced at Matt and Shawn. They both seemed to have missed the whole thing. She, too, let it go and put her eyes to her cookie.

Mavis read her fortune aloud. "Your future is very

bright, no matter what today might bring." Matt clapped her on the back, and then her friends took turns reading theirs.

Funny, but no matter what the fortune said, Mavis simply didn't see the light at the end of the tunnel.

CHAPTER 10

Detective Gordon sat at his desk once again, this time with the receiver to his desk phone propped between his ear and left shoulder. He was on hold, waiting for information on the family of one Aneta Shevchenko, mother of Shanice Hall. Her family hailed from Ukraine, and he needed a telephone number of anyone who was related to her. While he waited for the international telephone operator to return to the line, he impatiently tapped his ink pen rapidly on the blotter of the desk.

"Detective Gordon?" The operator's voice suddenly came out of nowhere, startling him back to reality.

"Yes, I'm here."

"Sir, I have countless listings under the name 'Shevchenko' all over Ukraine." The operator had a regretful tone to her voice. "In order for me to track down anything close to the number you are looking for, I am going to need a first name, or we'll never be able to narrow it down, sir."

Ben closed his eyes in frustration. "I understand. Let me do a bit more digging. Thank you for your help."

"You have a wonderful day sir," she concluded.

Ben hung up the phone and ran his hand through his hair, which was already tousled and standing on end. He sat back to think about his options regarding the situation. He had researched Aneta (Shevchenko) Hall fairly well, or so he had thought. From what he could gather, it appeared that Michael Hall had found her on some kind of mail-order bride ad years ago. He brought her to America, and the two married, having Shanice. But the magazine that ran the ad had no personal information on Aneta regarding her family. Suddenly, it came to him: the paper, which had gone under with the dawn of the Internet, had been based in the city of Odessa, Ukraine. Maybe, just maybe, he could narrow down Aneta's roots by starting in that town.

He began by calling Odessa's State Archival Service, which would have birth records for natural citizens there. Ben had no idea if Aneta had even been born in Odessa, where the paper had been, but it was yet another starting point. He put in the long-distance call.

After struggling momentarily with the language barrier, the woman on the other end of the line managed to get an English-speaking worker on the phone to answer his questions. Relieved, he got his pen and paper ready and introduced himself. Once most people, especially government workers, realized he was a police official, they typically gave him all the help he needed easily.

"I'm hoping you can help me," he began after the introduction. "Anton, I'm working on a murder case here in Ohio, USA, and I need to track down a witness who has pertinent information. However, she and her family seem to have simply disappeared. I discovered that the mother of the witness is from Ukraine, and some of the other information I gathered suggested she might have ties to Odessa, possibly might have even been born there. Are you able to check into this for me?"

Anton replied, "If you give me a name, I will check for birth records and other related records, officer."

"Aneta Shevchenko," he said.

"Hold please."

Strange music came over the line, signifying he was playing the waiting game again. Putting the call on speakerphone, he stood and filled his coffee cup, then returned to the desk and sat. Just seconds later, Anton was back on the line.

"Officer?"

Ben cleared his throat. "Yes, I'm here."

"I have located a certificate of birth in Odessa for one Aneta Shevchenko, born December 20, 1980. It appears, according to other records, that she went to the United States several years back, and gained citizenship there at one point. Could that be who you are looking for?"

"Yes, yes." He was starting to get both relieved and excited. "Could you tell me the name of her parents, please?"

"Certainly," Anton said. "Mother: Bodashka Shevchenko. Father: Boris Shevchenko. There is also a death record for the father from five years ago, but from what I can find the mother is still alive."

Ben sighed with relief. "I don't suppose you have any current contact information for the mother?"

"I'm sorry sir, I do not."

Ben thanked Anton and hung up briefly, then picked up the receiver and contacted international information once again.

"I need information for Odessa, Ukraine, please," he said to the male operator.

"Yes, go ahead sir."

Ben glanced down at his notes. "Address and telephone information for one Bodashka Shevchenko."

He could hear the man tapping away on a keyboard briefly, but it didn't take him long to give Ben just the information he was looking for.

"Shevchenko, Boris, and Bodashka... Number 20, Bunina Street... telephone number... Oh! You will need to dial 011 before the number if calling from the United States, sir."

After writing the information, Ben sat back, a grateful smile on his face. "You have no idea how much of a help you have been. Thank you so much."

"It's my pleasure," the man replied. "Have a wonderful day, and thank you for using International Information."

After disconnecting, Ben took the time to think about the path his conversation with this woman should take. She might not even be the mother of Aneta at all; after all, how many Aneta Shevchenkos might there be in Odessa, let alone all of Ukraine? Well, he was going to find out.

Time to give Mrs. Shevchenko a call.

After a long drink of coffee, Ben picked up the phone and began to dial the foreign number. She might not even be home, or she might be napping. He could hope that this would go smooth as silk, but the fact was that he had run into so many brick walls he just couldn't be sure. Ben Gordon braced himself to hit yet another, but he remained hopeful.

The phone rang three times when it was answered by an older woman who sounded tired and gruff. The static on the line was annoying, and he struggled to hear the hello she gave him in her native tongue. Oh, here was the brick wall he had been waiting for.

"Is this Mrs. Bodashka Shevchenko?"

"Ya… who dis?"

After clearing his throat one more time, Ben continued. "Mrs. Shevchenko, my name is Detective Benjamin Gordon from the United States. I am looking for your daughter, Aneta, and her family. They have some important information we need."

The woman on the other end of the phone went silent.

"Ma'am, are you still there?"

When she replied, her voice was even gruffer than before, bordering on rude. "I am here," she said. "What you want with Aneta? She no more lives in America… she and family start new. They are dead to the world, born new for a new life."

Ben was confused. Dead? Did the woman mean that

they had all been killed, or that they simply left their old lives behind? He was hoping for the latter.

"All three of them have passed away?" he asked, bracing himself for the answer.

The woman snorted into the phone. "I said nothing about 'passing away,' as you say. I say they are dead to the world. They have left all of the old behind, and they have started anew. Shanie needed to begin fresh, to learn new lessons, and that could not be done in your filthy country. They are in a new place, and I will not play a part in dragging their past into the present, Mr. Police Man."

The phone went dead in his hand.

"Mrs. Shevchenko?" Ben knew she had hung up on him, but he wanted to make sure. "Mrs. Shevchenko?"

After waiting several seconds, Ben hung up the phone and sat back in his chair to reflect on their short conversation. "Shanie," as the old woman had referenced, must have been Shanice. He could assume by all she said that the Halls had left the country, probably even changed their names, and likely would never return, all for the sake of escaping the past… but what would be bad enough to escape?

Murder, perhaps?

Determined to continue his search for the Halls, Ben Gordon scribbled down several pertinent notes, then made plans to visit Candy Wilkes once again. Now he had a tugging feeling that both girls might have been involved in all the killings. It didn't matter to him that Shanice and her family had moved to Cleveland; it wasn't too great a distance for her to travel back and help her friend get revenge on the one she hated so much. So, yes, he would keep up his search, but in the meantime, he was going to focus on putting a good amount of pressure on Shanice's sidekick. The girl whose mother had managed to make her look so innocent, but had failed to rid the girl of the evil inside of her heart and the terrible attitude that came with it.

Yes, the thing to do was focus on the here and now. But he would not stop looking for the missing girl or her family. He knew deep inside she had something to do with all of this, that Candy simply wouldn't have started such a mess on her own, even if she did continue on once her friend was gone.

(

CHAPTER 11

"Your Grandma Cabot is a card," Matt Morgan was saying to Mavis as she handed him a fresh bottle of water. "She makes me crack up laughing every time I see her."

The pair had just returned to Mavis' house after having Sunday dinner at her grandmother's. Her parents had stayed behind to finish up some yard work and play a game of cards outside in the cool of the day. The kids headed home to catch a movie, but mostly they left so Mavis could dig into some cow organs that Matt had managed to bring her from work. She had just finished eating and cleaning up, and now they were going to relax in front of the living room television set.

"I know," Mavis replied as she plopped down on the sofa next to her boyfriend. "She's been like that my whole life, probably longer. She's something else."

After a pause, Matt said, "You know, with her spunky attitude, it would have been interesting to have her with us at Chinese Chang's. I think she might have had plenty to say to Candy and her attitude."

Mavis hadn't filled Matt in on what Candy had said to her when they were sitting alone. She didn't want him to make a scene, or Kim for that matter and both of them had just the personality to do just that. Now, however, it seemed like telling him just came naturally.

"Speaking of Candy and Chang's, I didn't mention that she had a mouthful to say to me when you, Kim, and Shawn went to the buffet."

Matt turned to her and gave her the eye. "I knew it. So, what was it?"

For the next ten minutes, Mavis filled him in on the fact that Candy had told her that her life is dreadful, and it was all Mavis' fault. She let him know that Candy wanted to stand back and watch her suffer and that she was glad Mavis' friends were dead. She also told him about Candy brushing up against her chair when she left, and she let him know she hadn't responded, even a little. Matt sat and listened to her in stunned silence, his anger growing with each word she spoke. By the time she was finished, he was sitting on the very edge of the sofa, fuming.

"She actually said those things? Mavis, why didn't you say something to me right away? I would have put that little jerk in her place right there in that restaurant."

Mavis nodded. "That's exactly why I didn't."

Matt stood and began to pace back and forth; after a moment, he stopped and turned to her. "Well, guess what? Now you're going to call that cop, Gorgon, or whatever his name is."

"Gordon," Mavis muttered with a sigh. "I knew you were going to say that. What good is it going to do?"

"Fine, Detective Gordon. The good it will do is that

he needs to know everything to solve his case, and we need him to solve his case in your favor. You are going to call him right now and tell him all this." As he spoke, Mavis saw something like a sparkle in his eye. "This could be exactly the type of thing we need to get the entire focus off you when it comes to these killings. Don't you see that it couldn't be more perfect?"

Mavis thought about it for a minute, but it didn't take her long to see the light. He was right; Candy's words made her sound guilty, even though she wasn't. The whole point was for Mavis to be able to learn to get on with her life, right? Yes, Matt had a point, all right, even if it was dishonest and wrong. She was in such turmoil over all this. Mavis was beginning to wonder if she even knew herself anymore.

"Do you still have his card?" Matt asked.

Mavis nodded. "In my room on the vanity."

Jumping up, she made her way down the hall, retrieved the card from where she had tucked it into the mirror frame of the vanity, and took it back out to the living room. Matt was waiting there with the cordless landline phone in his hand. When Mavis sat next to him on the sofa, he handed the receiver over to her, and she dialed the number for Detective Ben Gordon.

She didn't expect the lawman to be in his office because it was Sunday. She voiced that to Matt, who insisted she call anyway. After all, she could leave a message for him to call her the following day if she had to. Defeated, Mavis went ahead and dialed the number. Much to her surprise, the phone rang twice, and then it was answered by the detective himself.

"Detective Gordon," he greeted.

Mavis took a deep breath. "Detective Gordon, this is Mavis Harvey. Um, I'm sorry to bother you on a Sunday. I was just planning to leave a message."

"No!" he replied quickly. "No problem. Cops like me really don't keep set hours, Mavis. How can I help you today?"

She proceeded to tell him about going to dinner at Chinese Chang's with her friends and her encounter with Candy Wilkes. Mavis filled him in on her bad attitude first, then told him all she had said when they were seated alone at their adjacent tables and how she had barged into her chair. Ben Gordon made agreeable noises at her every pause, and she knew he was quickly writing down every word she was saying. She felt miserable during the entire call. If what she was doing was so right, why did she feel so horrible?

When she was finished, he went over every detail twice, making sure he had all the information she had given him correct. When they were finished, he thanked her for the call, telling her that it was very helpful. Mavis wasn't so sure. Deep inside, she knew they were laying undue blame on the girl, even if she and Matt both thought it was for the best.

Mavis said, "Well, I don't want to get her into trouble if she really hasn't done anything." Matt gave her a gentle slug in the arm, and she stuck her tongue out. "I just thought it was weird, the things she said and all."

"Certainly," Gordon replied. "Don't feel bad, Mavis; you've done the right thing by calling me. Thank you very much, and try to not let her attitude and words get you down. Enjoy the rest of your Sunday as best you can, and I'll sort this out, okay?"

"Thank you, Detective."

With that, the call was disconnected.

"So, what did he say?" Matt asked.

Mavis shrugged, feeling badly about the little scheme. "He's going to sort it out, or look into it, or something. He said it was very helpful."

With a sigh and a smile, Matt snatched up the TV remote and sat back on the sofa. "Good. I'm telling you, it's all going to be all right. Remember, the girl is evil; what is supposed to happen, will."

As Matt chose a movie to watch, Mavis' mind swam around the call, Candy, and the murders that she had committed herself. Was it really right to let that mean girl take the fall for her actions? Well, hopefully, Matt wasn't too far off when he said that what was meant to be would be.

She just hoped that things worked out for the best for everyone, even Candy. No, especially Candy. The girl was a mess. She had to be, didn't she, to insinuate that she had done things she hadn't done? Did she deserve to be wrongly accused and condemned any more than the boys or her classmates deserved to die? No, she did not.

Mavis pretended to enjoy the movie, but throughout the entire picture, she did nothing but fret and worry.

That night, Mavis lay in her bed, tired and full from just having a couple of squirrels Matt had dropped off, surprising her, before heading to the packing house for work. Her room was dark and cozy, but she was wide awake, even in her exhaustion. She just couldn't get her mind off either the call to Detective Gordon or Candy Wilkes.

Suddenly, her cell phone began to vibrate on the nightstand next to her bed. Thinking it would be Matt or Kim, she snatched it up and looked at the screen. She didn't recognize the number specifically, but it was a Greenville number, so she answered without hesitation.

"Hello?"

"Mavis Harvey?"

Immediately, Mavis recognized the voice of Candy Wilkes, the sneer in her tone giving her away completely.

"What do you want, Candy?"

The girl paused. "Oh, not much. I just thought that, considering all the people who seem to die around you that you should keep a close eye on your little Goth boyfriend. For all any of us know, something terrible could happen to him too. Sweet dreams now, Mavie-Wavie!"

After a sickening laugh from Candy, the phone went dead in her hand. Mavis stared at the screen, then turned off the ringer and buried her face into her pillow to cry in silence.

Did Candy Wilkes know more about Mavis and her

little zombie problem than anyone thought? Now, Mavis was beginning to be convinced that the girl did. What if she had gone to Colin's house with malicious intent and saw Mavis chowing down on him right then and there? What if she was setting Mavis up bigger than ever, planning to spring the deadly information on her at the right time to destroy her? Mavis felt like throwing up; her imagination was working overtime, and her guilt didn't help matters at all.

She knew she would be lucky to get any sleep at all. If she had dreams, she was positive they wouldn't be pleasant. She was scared and worried, for the people in her life who cared about her and went to such great lengths to meet her needs and ensure her safety.

Mavis was in a great big mess. It wasn't legal, it was personal. It was a personal, moral crisis that she had no idea how to sort out. How does one deal with waking up one day and becoming a zombie? She had no idea, and there were no textbooks or classes at the community college to teach her what she needed to know. Sure, she and Matt were learning how to deal with the physical repercussions of the condition, but had both of them neglected to consider the emotional and mental? It certainly appeared to be so.

She sobbed into her pillow until she had nothing left to give. Still, she didn't sleep. Nothing she tried to do helped with shutting off her mind. She was exhausted, but she felt as though she would never sleep again. All her brain would do was think about "zombiehood," as she had come to call it in her own mind. Was there actually never a documented case of this kind of thing before that she could read about and learn from?

In an effort to wind down her own mind, Mavis grabbed her smartphone and began to search, looking for even the slightest hint that she wasn't alone. She obsessed there, alone in her room by the light of the phone, for nearly the entire night. It wasn't until the crack of dawn and the first chirping of birds that she realized she had another sleepless night and her heart was still broken.

Something had to give. Something had to happen to help her feel better about who she had become on the outside, and how she could deal with it on the inside. The bottom line was this: Mavis felt utterly broken and alone, no matter who she had in her life to help her through it.

She was going to do what Matt would want her to do, no matter how she felt; she would call Gordon the next morning and report the call. Harassment was harassment, after all. Mavis just wanted it to end.

CHAPTER 12

At exactly 10:13 the following morning, Ben Gordon hung up the phone in his office and rested his chin on steepled fingers. The caller he had just disconnected from had been none other than Mavis Harvey, calling for the second time in less than twenty-four hours. Once again, the poor girl had received a call from Candy Wilkes, and once again, it was less than pleasant. From the way it sounded, it was downright menacing and threatening.

Gordon advised her to begin to record any future calls, not to avoid them, as she understandably wanted to do. Mavis had agreed, thanking him for his help. The calls enraged Ben, while also increasing his suspicions regarding Candy and Shanice by leaps and bounds.

Sure, Shanice Hall had moved to Cleveland, but before she virtually disappeared, she could easily have had a hand in the deaths of both Jeff Deason and Colin Handley. Yes, she was long gone by the time the prom murders took place, but little Miss Candy was still around. Could she really have carried out such a dastardly and terrible crime on her own? He didn't see how, but if there was one thing he had learned in all of his years policing and detecting, it was that even the most unlikely of suspects could accomplish almost anything they put their minds to. He was going to keep his focus on Candy Wilkes, and he was going to put the pressure on her heavier than ever.

Ben made some detailed notes regarding the call he had just received from Mavis while they were fresh in his mind. When he was finished, he stood up, straightened his tie, and grabbed his suit coat and notebook. Time to pay yet another visit to Candy and her mother. It was time to start getting some kind of answers that made sense, even if he had to drag them out of her.

He left, closing his office behind him, determination on his face and in his step. Yes, he had himself convinced that Candy was guilty at one level or another. But even if she wasn't, what she was putting the Harvey girl through was wrong, and he wasn't going to allow it to continue.

People confused him. How could some have a perfect life, and turn out so bad, while others grew up with nothing but neglect and abuse, and rose above it? The bottom line was that people were usually bad seeds, most of them selfish and unpredictable. That's why there were cops; someone had to protect those who didn't deserve the crap dealt to them by others. As he went, he became even more determined to get to the bottom of the case, before any more damage was done.

∞

"Mavis, the truth is, it seems like Candy's doing this

on purpose; she's doing it to herself." Matt watched her eat a bit of cow intestine on the garbage bags on her bedroom floor. "I mean, it's almost like she wants credit for the deaths, you know what I mean?"

Mavis nodded and tore off a piece of intestine, slurping it into her mouth expertly.

The action didn't faze Matt at all; he was more than accepting of Mavis and all that she was. His concern was keeping her safe and secure. None of this was her fault, or at least, none of it was done with malice or intent. If anyone in authority were to find out what she was, there would be a major mess. They likely wouldn't put her in prison, but they would lock her up to study her at the very least, and who knew what kind of torment she would have to endure. Not to mention that the worst-case scenario would involve her being dissected. No, he had to help keep her safe; he loved her, and he felt it was his duty.

Mavis put the last shred of intestine into her mouth and began to furiously pluck baby wipes out of the box next to her. She began to glance around, making sure she had gotten no blood or tissue on anything other than the bags. Satisfied, she stood, finished cleaning her face and hands as best as she could, and started rolling up the taped-up bags for disposal.

Matt sat forward, watching her work. "Maybe we could do something to move things along a little."

Mavis stopped and turned to him, narrowing her eyes at him. "What do you mean, Matthew?"

Matt got a sheepish look on his face and shrugged.

"I don't know… I guess I meant that maybe we could do something that kind of… makes her look guilty."

"No, Matthew! How could you even think that way?" Mavis' white skin almost took on a red-hue, she was so angry. "That would lower us to her level, and I'm not doing it!"

She sat down on the bed next to him and calmed her voice. "Listen, the fact is: I'm the one who did these things. While I'm not going to come out and admit it, I'm also not going to intentionally blame someone else. If Candy gets into trouble for all this because of her own behavior, that's one thing. Setting her up to take a fall for me is another altogether."

"You're right," he said. "Sorry. If she hangs, she'll hang herself."

"Exactly."

The pair stood up and gathered the rolled-up garbage bags, tucked them into a new one, and knotted it up for disposal. Todd was at work, and Mavis' mother, Jane, was volunteering at the homeless shelter, so taking out the "trash" would be easy.

After letting Feisty out to go potty, Mavis locked up the house and met Matt out at his car. She climbed into the passenger side and buckled up while he put the garbage bag securely in the trunk, then he got in beside her and started the vehicle.

As they pulled away, Mavis turned to him, concern on her face. "Matt, why do you think Candy is doing this? I mean, why would she want to look guilty? After her call last night, I was sort of scared she knew about me for some reason."

"Well," he began, "I don't think she has a clue about you, first of all. Secondly, I think she is so furious about having to go to Juvic, and then losing her best friend because of the situation, that watching you squirm and hurt makes her feel better. Maybe she wants you to think she did those things because it gives her a sense of retribution."

"What kind of person does something like that?" she asked.

Matt gave her a sympathetic look. "A sick one, Mav. A very sick one."

The two drove off, heading for a dumpster with the garbage bag. Everything Matt said made sense, but she still couldn't comprehend the type of thinking that Candy seemed to possess. Mavis might be a zombie, but she hated to see other people hurt, and the things she had done since getting "sick" made her nauseous.

Zombie or not, she was thankful she wasn't so angry and hateful inside. Not that she understood how the two were separated from each other; one would think that they would go hand in hand. Here she was, a flesh-eating zombie who had a guilt complex about eating people, while some girl across town, raised in a religious home, was doing all she could to make Mavis' life miserable; who could figure it?

No one and that was the reality of the situation. Even though she was scared about the future, she was glad that Ben Gordon was on the case. Even in her fear, it gave her someone to turn to who wasn't going to let her get pushed around, and he had the law of the land to back him up. It was truly a relief.

Letting him do what he had to do was the best idea for everyone involved.

CHAPTER 13

"I don't care how it makes her feel. If it weren't for Mavis Harvey, I wouldn't be stuck in this stupid house all day, every day. If it weren't for her, Shanice would still be here. I hope she's scared and hurt. I hope she's worried about what I'll do, even if I do nothing. If you want the truth, I hope she dies and rots!"

Candy Wilkes shot an evil look at her mother, who was nearly in tears. She then turned her eyes back to Ben Gordon, who was jotting down her words as fast as he could. This girl was a piece of work, all right. She seemed to have no compassion, no ability to think outside of her own selfish little bubble. He shot a quick glance at Mrs. Wilkes, who was blushing with embarrassment and shame. She looked as though she was on the verge of crying, and this made Ben Gordon angry. What was wrong with kids nowadays? This kind of young person made him fear for the state of their country. They were going to be running things someday.

He met Candy's blazing eyes. "Is your life really so bad, young lady? Look around you for a moment, would you? It could be so, so much worse. If you or Shanice, or both of you, had anything to do with these murders at all, you could go to prison for the rest of your life. I don't think you appreciate the gravity of this situation at all, or that you fully comprehend the kind of trouble you are in! Here you are, being questioned regarding serious crimes, and you're staying up at night to prank call the very person you victimized in the first place! What is the matter with you, anyway?"

Candy simply shrugged; her mother let out an audible sob.

With a disgusted shake of his head, Ben continued. "You know, your mother and father have made choices regarding your life in an effort to help you, to give you a future, and to put the past behind you so you can be happy. But from the things you allegedly said to Mavis in the restaurant and on the phone, you could care less." He paused. "Candy Wilkes, did you have anything to do with the deaths of the boys or those at the prom?"

Candy didn't miss a beat. "If you think I did, why don't you figure it out?"

He was so angry and disgusted with the innocently-dressed girl that he was nearly shaking. Ben wanted to grab her around her scrawny little neck and squeeze. He wanted to turn her over his knee and paddle her butt with a board until she got the lesson drilled into her. But Ben knew that this girl was past all of that; there was something seriously bad inside of her, and it reeked of disregard and cruelty. No wonder she and Shanice had been best friends.

He turned his attention to his pad and wrote down her answer, then gave Mrs. Wilkes a look of pity. The woman now had tears running down her face. The kid made him sick! If any of his kids acted like her, they wouldn't have lived long, he could tell her that, but he held his tongue.

Ben stood up. "Well, those are, indeed, my suspicions. If you did anything or was involved in those killings in even the most remote of ways, I will figure it out, and I will prove it." To Mrs. Wilkes, he said, "Ma'am, you might want to get an attorney for your daughter whether she is guilty or innocent. I am going to be talking to her more, much more unless I find evidence to disprove my suspicions. Oh, and ma'am? I am so very sorry you have had to live with this behavior at all." He glanced at Candy just in time to see the girl shoot a smirk of hatred at him; he was fuming.

Ben drained the glass of lemonade Mrs. Wilkes had gotten for him, thanked her, and left. As he made his way back to the freeway in his car, he thought briefly about Shanice Hall. If these two girls had done these crimes, he was pretty sure that the missing Shanice had been the mastermind. Ben was losing sleep consistently trying to find the Hall family, but it was as if they had taken a rocket ship into space with no plan to return. They had somehow disappeared into the mist, and without her, he would never know the truth.

Suddenly, a thought flashed through his mind: Mrs. Shevchenko said dead to the world. What if Candy had killed off the Hall family? Was it possible? Maybe she had done it to save her own rear-end!

Ben laughed aloud, long and hard. That was

ridiculous! How would she have disposed of the bodies and taken care of their possessions? No, that wasn't it; the Halls couldn't be found because they didn't want to be, and that just solidified his suspicions that the two girls were involved in all the murders.

He turned his car onto the freeway and thought out the crimes as he thought they might have happened.

The first killing was Jeffrey Deason, the star football player. It was Ben's thought that the kid never intended to stand Mavis up for the Homecoming Dance. His theory was that the boy was actually either on his way to get her, and ran into Shanice or Candy, or both. Maybe they asked him for a ride, maybe he offered. Either way, Ben Gordon believed they got into his car, and once they were in, he was a dead man. It likely would have taken both the girls to burn the evidence the way it had been burned, or one large person. He thought it was likely two, though.

That brought him to Colin Handley. This young man was found dead and mutilated in his parents' home. It was easy for Ben to assume that the girls showed up at his door before he even had a chance to leave to pick up his date for the Winter Formal. They had slaughtered him, acts a sick adult could think up and carry out. But together it would have been simple. Man, this was a couple of sick girls, if they indeed were the killers. They had even left the mess for his parents to find. Also, that was a murder that Candy could have done alone if Shanice hadn't been around. It wasn't unthinkable, anyway. Either way, he was sure she had something to do with it directly.

But the Junior Prom murders were an entirely different story. Shanice would have been gone, at least to Cleveland, by then. Maybe she snuck back to Greenville to assist, but even if that was the case, how did they manage to massacre all those people without someone stopping them in the act? This was his point of confusion because the entire mass murder took place in a locked gymnasium. The police had found the escape hatch, and it was assumed by all that the perp escaped through there. Due to emergency drills, the fingerprints of every student and teacher were in the vicinity of the hidden hatch, so that was sort of worthless evidence. But how did they overpower so many people, most of whom were larger and stronger than they were?

As he drove, his mind continued to race with these unanswered questions. That's when it hit him: hadn't Mr. Hall, Shanice's father, been some kind of doctor, maybe even a surgeon? Yes! He'd had a small practice in Toledo for years. The idea was a stretch, but what if Shanice and Candy had managed to get their hands on some kind of gaseous anesthetic, like sleeping gas, or something similar? What if they had worn masks while hiding by the hatch, released the gas into the air, and then went about committing their grisly crimes? Likely they had intended Mavis and Matt to be their only victims, not knowing that the kids had skipped the event. If this had been the scenario, why did they tear the whole junior class apart?

Maybe, to them, it was all fun and games.

It was only a theory about the Junior Prom and his two suspects, but for now, it was something. Time to get to the office and track down anyone who had worked for or with Mr. Hall when he was in practice. Maybe he could get information from one of them about the family's whereabouts, and maybe he would learn more than he could imagine.

Ben punched the gas and steered up the freeway with newfound purpose.

CHAPTER 14

Tuesday afternoon was to be a productive time for Mavis and Jane, as well as Matt. After he woke from sleeping after his night-shift job, he made his way to the Harvey house to help with yard work. By two, Matt was mowing, Jane and Mavis were weeding the flower beds, and Feisty was running around being worthless like a dog should.

When they first started the weeding, Jane had attempted to speak with her daughter about the situation with Candy Wilkes. She knew about the prank call, but Mavis had said nothing to her about the confrontation at Chinese Chang's. Mavis knew if the threats appeared to be an ongoing pattern, Jane would have a conniption, and that was something no one wanted to deal with. When her mother broached the subject, Mavis reassured her that she had contacted Detective Gordon, and he was taking care of everything. Jane's eyes said she didn't buy it, but the woman wisely let the subject drop.

The conversation ended up consisting of chatter about Kim and Shawn, and how their relationship was going. This morphed into a talk about Matt, and how he and Mavis were getting along. Jane spent a lot of time praising the young man. It seemed that his dark, Gothic appearance was invisible to her parents. Jane let her daughter know that she believed the boy's feelings for Mavis were deep and genuine, and she also bragged him up for his constant willingness to help the family out, which made him seem like a part of the family that had been around forever. This made Mavis happy; she was truly in love with the boy who loved her, even in all her zombie glory.

There was a brief lull in the conversation as they continued to pluck weeds. Suddenly, Jane stopped and looked up at Mavis with a slightly stricken expression. Mavis looked at her and waited.

"Oh, my! I forgot to check the mail today! Your father has very important documents coming from a private client, and I was supposed to make sure to take them to him to sign right away so he could mail them out today!"

Without further words, Jane jumped up and ran for the house, leaving the sliding glass door open in her rush. Matt stopped the mower and went to the patio to have a drink of his soda. He took a gulp and turned to Mavis.

"What's up with her?" he asked.

Mavis plucked a massive dandelion weed. "She forgot to check the mail; something important for my dad."

No sooner were the words out of her mouth than a shrill scream rang out from the front yard. Matt literally dropped his plastic tumbler to the ground and took off for the front like a shot. Mavis was right on his heels. Why was her mother screaming bloody murder?

Both Mavis and Matt darted through the sliding glass door, through the house, and out the front entrance. Mrs. Dandridge, their neighbor to the right, was also running toward Jane, as was Mr. Hughes from across the street.

Jane was standing at the mailbox by the curb. The door to the box was open, and she was staring inside, still screaming at the top of her lungs. Her face was white as a ghost, and from Mavis' point of view, it looked like her mother had tears running down her face.

Matt reached the hysterical woman first, so he put his hand on her arm and asked, "What is it, Mrs. Harvey?"

Jane simply pointed at the box with a trembling hand and let out another scream. By that time, Mavis reached them, and both she and Matt looked into the box. What they saw shook up both of them, but not enough to scream.

"Mrs. Dandridge, will you please take my mother into the house?"

As Mavis asked the woman for the favor, she closed the box quickly. Mrs. Dandridge didn't hesitate, putting her arm around Jane's trembling form and leading her back inside. Mr. Hughes reached the kids at that point.

"What is going on, kids?" he asked in his famous gruff voice.

Matt opened the box to show him. Inside, on top of

a pile of letters, sat what appeared to be a doll. Matt removed it so they could get a better look.

It was a Matt Doll. The figure was dressed all in black, with stark white face and hands, and exaggerated circles of eyeliner around huge saucer-shaped eyes. It was just small enough to fit into the box. But the fact that it was a Matt Doll wasn't what was so disturbing; the scary part was that it had a knife sticking out of his chest, and what appeared to be red food coloring was smeared all over it. Someone had even drawn little bite marks in black on his face, neck, and hands.

"Oh, my?" Mr. Hughes muttered. "Is that supposed to be you?"

Matt looked up at Mavis, then at the neighbor. "I'm afraid so, Mr. Hughes. I'm afraid so."

∞

Matt sat silently in Todd's recliner, staring at the crude, horrid-looking doll, which he held in his hands. Mavis sat on the couch with her mother, one arm protectively around the woman's shoulders as she calmed her with soothing, reassuring words. Jane was no longer crying, but she was still pretty shaken up.

Todd was on his way home from the office to be with his wife, thanks to a quick call and explanation from Mavis. Ben Gordon was also on his way, thanks to Matt, who had taken the liberty of calling the detective from his cell. Now, as he sat and stared at the smaller, bloodier rendition of himself, he felt his anger growing. How dare someone do this? The upset it had caused Jane was ridiculous, but Matt also knew that Mavis was furious. It was going to be difficult to convince her that she didn't need to take matters into her own hands with Candy Wilkes after this.

All of them were sure it had been Candy; after all, who else could it have been? This morbid, sick attempt at a joke was more like a passive-aggressive threat, and both Mavis and Matt took it strictly as such. Even though they both knew the truth about the murders, this girl was taking things to another level. Matt even thought that Mavis might have been right when she suggested that Candy knew about her zombie state. Well, maybe not the zombie part, but perhaps she knew about Mavis' involvement after all.

There was a brisk knock on the door, which they all knew would be Ben Gordon. Matt set the doll on the end table and jumped up to answer it; Mavis thanked him with her eyes and continued to soothe her mom. In seconds, Ben was in the living room, doll in hand, and he was furious.

The first words out of his mouth when he laid eyes on the thing were, "I think we can safely say this has gone to the next level."

Jane, though still shaken, was more than happy to get her mind off the incident and play hostess, offering Ben soda or tea. He accepted, and she disappeared into the kitchen while he took a seat on the sofa next to Mavis. Whipping out his pen and pad, he looked at both of the kids, his look serious and determined.

"Tell me exactly what happened," he said.

Matt replied first, his voice low and more serious

than Mavis had ever heard before. "We were doing yard work, the three of us. I was mowing, and the girls were weeding."

Mavis added, "Mom stopped all of a sudden and said she had forgotten to check the mail; something important was coming for Dad, and it had to be taken to him before the day was over. She ran through the back door and through the house to go to the mailbox."

As if on cue, Todd came through the front door. Ben immediately stood and shook his hand, then the two men sat down. Ben was the one to fill Todd in on what he had missed, then the conversation continued while Jane brought glasses of tea.

"Anyway," Matt continued, picking up where they had left off while Jane went to get a drink for her husband, "I turned the mower off so I could take a drink of soda. I asked Mavis where her mom went, she told me, and then Jane screamed like no other."

Ben scribbled furiously in his pad. "What did you both do next?"

"We ran for the house to see what happened," Mavis replied. "It sounded like she was hurt, or being attacked, or something. So, we ran through the house and out the front door, and there she was, standing at the mailbox, screaming bloody murder. She was just staring inside of the box like she was in shock."

Matt added, "A couple of neighbors came, too. Mr. Hughes and Mrs. Dandridge, but they went home when she started to calm down a bit."

Todd's face was turning red. "I'd like to see the doll,

please."

Ben had put the doll into a bag, considering it as evidence. He handed it to Todd and said, "Sorry, sir. But I'll have to take it when I leave."

Todd nodded and looked at the macabre thing through the plastic, gently turning it over a few times in his hands before shaking his head and handing it back to Ben Gordon. He growled slightly, showing more anger than Mavis had ever seen him show. Jane entered the room with Todd's tea, then took a seat in her rocker.

"I consider this to be a threat," Todd said in a low voice, "I consider it to be emotional assault. What can be done about this?"

Ben cleared his throat and set the doll next to him. "Well, I'm pretty sure we all have clear suspicions regarding who is responsible for this. But legally we need to be sure. The first thing I'll do is take the report; next, I'll speak directly to the suspect, and the lab will give the doll a good going over. This is necessary if we want to be able to tie the doll to the suspect. You know, they'll search for fingerprints and the like. Depending on what we come up with, if the suspect is the culprit, you can press charges, and that person will be arrested for harassment."

"This is just insane," Todd said forcefully.

Ben nodded. "Mrs. Harvey, do you have a legal pad or a notebook with lined paper? I'll need each of you to write, in detail, your own version of events. This excludes you, of course, Mr. Harvey."

Todd stood up. "I have one in my briefcase. It's in the car; I'll be right back."

The next hour was spent writing down their individual stories, then Ben took the doll, told them all to keep their doors locked, and to in no way seek retribution or take the law into their own hands. Finally, he left, but Mavis, Matt, and her parents sat in silence for some time. No one could believe all that was happening, especially Mavis.

After all, the truth was that it was all her fault, every last bit of it.

CHAPTER 15

The first thing Detective Gordon did when he got back to his office was to type up the reports and attach the original handwritten ones appropriately. He would have to have Matthew Morgan and the Harvey ladies sign the official ones the next day. Once that was finished, he postponed his plan to search for Dr. Hill's employees. The situation with the Harveys and the doll had to take precedence.

He tucked the reports into the folder designated for Candace Wilkes and left once again, this time to return to the Wilkes home for another talk with Miss Attitude. While he drove, Ben practiced a lot of calming self-talk and breathing exercises; he was angry that this girl had such audacity, but he had to maintain control. After all, she might not have been the one to leave the doll in the mailbox. She didn't drive, and it was a fairly good trip between the two girls' homes. Regardless, when a person set their mind on something, nothing could stop them, especially angry, dysfunctional people like Candy Wilkes.

When he pulled up to the curb outside of Candy's home, the first thing he saw was the girl and her mother working in the front yard. Both wore ankle-length skirts and light t-shirts, and both wore ponytails in their hair; they were sweating profusely. Ben tucked the bagged doll into his briefcase gently, got out of the car, and started up the walk.

When Mrs. Wilkes saw him, a look of defeat came over her face. "Good afternoon, Detective."

"Good afternoon, Mrs. Wilkes," he replied pleasantly. "It's a warm one today; perfect for working in the yard."

"Yes." Her tone was curt but pleasant; her expression didn't match at all. She was frustrated at his presence.

Candy stopped what she was doing and just glared at him, then rolled her eyes. "What now?"

Ben maintained a smile. "We should probably talk in the house; it would be more comfortable for both of you." He glanced around at the neighboring houses to get his point across.

"Does it really matter?" Candy asked. "We don't want to talk to you anyway."

With a cluck of his tongue, he replied, "We can go to the station if you like."

Candy groaned loudly and stomped her bare feet as she made her way to the front door. Mrs. Wilkes was barefoot as well, and she followed her daughter much more gingerly, as though her feet ached. Ben Gordon let them lead the way.

This time there were no offers for tea or lemonade; they didn't even ask him to have a seat, though both of them sat as soon as they were inside. So, rather than make himself at home, Ben simply stood where he was, the smile still on his face, his briefcase in hand.

Candy looked at him smugly. "Well?"

"Have you been home all day today, Candy?" he asked, getting right to the point.

Mrs. Wilkes jumped in, answering for her daughter. "We did a bit of shopping together."

Ben continued to direct his words at the Wilkes girl. "Where did you shop, Candy?"

After looking slyly at her mother out of the corner of her eye, she said, "At Shop-A-Lot for groceries. Then we went to pick up some new summer clothes, you know, some looser, cooler stuff. We got these skirts, actually."

Now Detective Gordon turned to the mother. "Where all did you shop, Mrs. Wilkes?"

The woman hesitated, looking briefly at her daughter with worry on her face. "In Greenville… at the strip mall on Davis Avenue."

Ben was pleased; Davis Avenue was very close to the Harvey house.

"May I sit down please?" he asked.

Mrs. Wilkes nodded but didn't speak, so he sat in the same place he sat each time he was there. "So, Candy, did you happen to… how should I say… get away from your mother for a short time?"

The girl shrugged and pretended to pick something off her skirt. "I don't remember. I think I went to the bathroom once."

"How long were you apart?"

Candy glared at him. "I don't know; I don't time myself when I pee, do you?"

He turned to the mother. "How long, Mrs. Wilkes?"

The woman studied her daughter for a moment, then turned fully to Ben. "Yes, she went to the bathroom, but then she went for a soda at the fast-food place across the street. She was gone probably twenty minutes."

Ben had to hide his pleasure; this was looking good. "When did you both get home?"

"I'm not sure," the woman said, pondering. "An hour or two ago."

Perfect, Ben thought.

He cleared his throat and crossed his arms over his chest. "Tell me, Candy. Are you into arts and crafts? I mean, are you the crafty type?"

Now her eyes left him, and she began to pick nervously at the arm of the loveseat where she sat. "I guess I like to tinker around with art a little."

Mrs. Wilkes' face broke out in a proud smile. "She likes to make dolls. Oh, she can make some of the cutest little dolls! Sometimes we even sell them at our church bazaar!"

"Mother!" Candy almost screeched the word, causing her mother to jump and her face to go white.

"What?" Mrs. Wilkes was genuinely confused. "What did I say wrong? You do make wonderful dolls, Candy." She turned to Ben. "What is this all about?"

That was his cue. Ben reached down and retrieved

his case from the floor and placed it on the sofa next to him. Popping the latches, he took the plastic-covered doll from inside, then sat and looked it over for effect. He could feel Mrs. Wilkes staring, and he could also feel the frightened and nervous vibes coming from her daughter.

"Dolls are interesting," he began. "I mean, if someone mentions a doll, the first thing I think of is a baby doll, like the kind little girls like to play with. But there are so many other types of dolls. There are Russian nesting dolls, rag dolls, paper dolls…"

"What is your point, Detective Gordon?" Mrs. Wilkes' voice was trembling a bit, and it made him feel sorry for her.

"I'm getting to that," he replied. "Like I said, there are tons of different kinds of dolls, and some of them are really weird. Like voodoo dolls. Have you ever seen a voodoo doll? I haven't, not personally, but in pictures, they're some of the creepiest things." He looked up at Candy. "What kind of dolls do you make?"

She shrugged.

"I'll bet you know quite a bit about dolls, if you make them, huh, Candy?" he asked.

"I know enough." She was still picking intently at the arm of the couch.

Now his smile broadened. "Really? That's great. Maybe you can tell me what kind of doll this is."

Ben stood and walked over to the sofa and sat down next to her. He held the bagged doll up to show her, but she didn't even bother to shift her eyes toward it. Now she was picking furiously.

"Candy, look at the doll," Mrs. Wilkes said, a definite edge to her voice.

The girl gave the doll a glance, then looked back to her picking. "Looks like some kind of simple, homemade doll."

"Hmmm." Ben thought about her answer. "That's funny because it looks like something out of a horror movie to me. Look, Mrs. Wilkes, maybe you know if this is a specific type of doll."

Ben held the doll out to her, and she took it gently into both hands. The woman looked at it for several moments, tears welling up in her eyes. Something was about to give, Ben was sure of it.

"Well, I'll tell you," Mrs. Wilkes began. "From what I've been told, it's a lookalike doll. The kind one would make for a friend, the kind representing someone a friend might love, like a keepsake." She shifted her gaze to Candy and then began to stare hard at her daughter. "But I certainly wouldn't think a knife in the chest, or fake blood, or bite marks, are something one who was making a keepsake gift would add to the project."

Ben nodded. "Not unless it wasn't supposed to be a keepsake at all."

The room was quiet for a long moment; Ben took the doll back and took it over to his case, where he put it safely away. He sat back down and waited for either of the females to speak first. Mrs. Wilkes broke the ice, speaking to him while maintaining the stare she held on her picking daughter.

"Candy made that doll; she told me it was a sort of apology gift for that girl Mavis." Candy squirmed uncomfortably. "She said it was Mavis' boyfriend. Candy, how could you? I thought that after we settled the prank call issue, this nonsense was going to stop. I'm starting to think that maybe you are a little deeper into this mess than I'd like to believe!"

Candy continued to pull and pick at the couch, sneering, but saying nothing.

"So, I take it you made the doll, and you delivered it yourself today while you were shopping," Ben stated matter-of-factly. "Is that correct?"

Candy whispered. "I suppose."

"Does this mean you intend to harm her boyfriend?" he asked. "The way you harmed Jeff Deason and Colin Handley?"

Candy jumped up, red-faced with rage. "Think whatever you want! Do whatever you want! Arrest me if you want, I don't care. I didn't kill those boys, but I wish I had! I'll tell you another thing, knowing Mavis Harvey's track record, this one will die too!"

Ben sighed. "I won't be arresting you today, but I am going to ticket you for harassment, and you'll have to go to court over it. I am going to advise the Harveys that they obtain an order of protection, which will keep you at least five-hundred feet from the Harveys at all times, not just Mavis, and it will include no calls or letters. If you break the order, you will find yourself back in Juvie so fast it will make your head spin."

Ben pulled his ticket book out of his case and began

to fill out the top page. "I'm sorry for all this, Mrs. Wilkes, but it seems this is the only course of action for now. As for you, Candy, I do believe you know something about the murders… all of them. I am actively seeking that proof you have challenged me to find."

Ten minutes later, Ben Gordon was on his way back to Greenville. It was past quitting time, but he wouldn't be going home any time soon. He would be at the office, pumping coffee into his body and trying to find employees of Shanice's father. Now was the time to start making the connections that seemed invisible.

CHAPTER 16

At seven the following morning, Detective Gordon was still at the office, clothing mussed and pouring a cup of coffee from the seventh pot of the night. Another all-nighter had been difficult, but fruitful. Ben had managed to track down two nurses and the physician's assistant who had worked at his Greenville practice before the Halls had left for Cleveland.

In a half-hour, he would start dialing the phone; in the meantime, he would make use of the officers' shower room and the extra suit he kept in his locker for times like this. First, he put in a quick call to his wife, who sounded like she was just waking. He apologized and gushed at her, but it did nothing for his guilt. Mentally, he made a note to send her a dozen roses when the florists opened.

In record time, he was cleaned up and rearing to start making his phone calls. With a fresh cup of java, Ben sat at his desk and gave his list of names and numbers a good once over. He would start with Karen Hartwig, the woman who had been Dr. Michael Hall's primary physician's assistant for twelve years. From his research, Ben learned that when the doctor and his family had relocated to Cleveland she, too, had moved to that city. But it had been a brief stay, and then she returned, even moving back to the same address where she had lived before leaving. Now, Karen was back in Greenville, living on a small residential street about five blocks from the Harvey place.

He slugged back some coffee, picked up the phone, and dialed.

On the second ring, a tired woman answered the phone with slurred words.

"Hello?"

"Good morning," Ben began. "Is this Karen Hartwig?"

She grunted. "Yeah, but I don't want any."

The woman was going to hang up, he knew, mistaking him for a telemarketer, so he hurried with his words.

"Ms. Hartwig, I'm Detective Ben Gordon with the Greenville Police Department's Homicide Division. I need to speak with you regarding a former employer of yours, Dr. Michael Hall."

Silence met him in return, but he could make out television sounds in the background; she was still on the line, so he patiently waited.

"What ya wanna talk to me 'bout him for?"

Ben winced… the woman was drunk, and the first thing in the morning, at that!

"Ms. Hartwig, it would be easier if we spoke in person," he said simply.

She hesitated. "Um, I dunno…"

"You're not in any trouble, ma'am," he reassured. "I just have some questions regarding an incident that took place with his daughter, Shanice. I promise I won't take up much of your time."

"Shanice? That li'l brat?" The woman gave a sloppy laugh. "I'm not surprised."

Ben ignored her. "Do you have time to let me stop by this morning?"

"Well, I s'pose," she stammered. "But make it snappy, 'kay? I got things to do."

He didn't waste any time. Verifying her address, Ben hung up and gathered his things. On the way out of the office, he dropped off the Matt doll, along with the appropriate paperwork, at the evidence room and signed the proper paperwork. In a short time, he was driving to Pearl Street to meet a very intoxicated Karen Hartwig, PA.

Karen lived in a small bungalow, which Ben could tell had probably been very cute and well-kept at one time, even up until recent months. The most obvious signs of neglect were the landscaping and house paint, but he could tell these had been let go for a period of a few months instead of years. The grass itself had been recently mowed but was still way overdue for attention.

Once on the porch, he took note of a small pile of rolled newspapers that had been ignored. A mail slot in the door explained the absence of an overstuffed box, but Ben fully expected to see all of her mail, unopened and unread, stacked or pushed aside on the other side. Whatever the woman had gone through had really managed to put her through the wringer. After all, she had maintained a seemingly flawless professional career for years, and now she was soused during the early morning hours. Karen Hartwig was trying to numb something.

Ben rang the bell, waited, rang again, and got no response. Noting that he hadn't heard an echo of a ring from outside, he gave a standard five-rap cop knock and listened for any sign of life. He got one in seconds.

"I'm comin'! Jeez! You knock like the cops!"

He heard Karen flip a single lock and the door flung open. There she stood in a torn fuzzy blue bathrobe that barely covered a knee-length nightgown with what appeared to be chili on the front. Her short brown hair was standing all over the place, and it looked like she might have slept on the right side of her head in the same chili that was on the front of her gown. Karen reeked of booze and cigarettes; in fact, one was dangling obscenely from the corner of her mouth. Ben reminded himself to breathe through his mouth because he was sure she didn't smell too friendly.

"That's because I am a cop," he greeted, holding his hand out. "Detective Ben Gordon, remember?"

Karen squinted her eyes as she tried to recall where she had heard that name before, then it dawned on her all at once, and she began to cackle like a chicken at her own alcohol-induced memory loss.

"Yeah, yeah… come on in." She opened the door to let him through and stood aside. "Do you want a drink? I might have a little bourbon somewhere…"

Suddenly, he remembered that he had brought two covered styrofoam cups of black tar coffee from the station with him, one especially for her. "You know what, I brought coffee; you wait right here… don't go away!"

Ben jogged back out to the car and fetched the still-piping hot beverages from the cup holder and locked the vehicle with his key fob. He returned to Karen, who stood looking like she might pass out against the door jamb. Stepping inside, he put one cup down, took the lid off the other, and helped get the lip of the cup to her mouth.

"Taste this… slow, slow! It's hot!"

One sip confirmed his warning, and her head jerked back in surprise. Ben, being a persistent devil, continued to encourage her, and after a couple of drinks, her eyes were beginning to open up all the way. He had a lot of cop friends with booze problems; this wasn't his first rodeo.

"Karen, why don't you sit in your favorite chair and take this cup," he suggested.

She didn't argue. Plopping herself down in a torn, overstuffed chair that matched none of the other furniture, she took the cup from Ben, wincing a bit as the heat came into contact with her fingers. She started to sip at it once again while Ben grabbed his own cup and made his way to a shabby loveseat, which did match the couch. The loveseat was covered with the mail that couldn't be seen from the porch, and he smiled to himself as he pushed it aside and had a seat.

The two drank their coffee in silence for several minutes. At last, Ben set his on an end table and set his focus on her; she was coming around. He needed her as lucid as possible.

"Do you have a coffee maker?" he asked. "I just love coffee."

She knit her brow. "Yeah, it's on the counter over there... somewhere. Coffee is in the canister. Sorry, you're gonna have to help yourself."

So, he did. He whipped up a pot, which was done in ten minutes. Fortunately, he found a large ceramic mug in the grimy dish strainer, rinsed it out, and filled it. When he took it to Karen, whose first cup was gone, she gratefully accepted it.

Ben sat back down, took a drink of his own cup, got out his trusty pad and pen, and turned to see her staring at him suspiciously.

"So, what's this all about, anyway?" she asked. "You said something 'bout Shanice Hall. I don't know what kind of help I can be, but I'll try. She in trouble or something?"

Ben smiled and flipped open his pad; good cops never gave away too much information, not if they wanted to find the answers they were looking for.

"I wouldn't say that," he replied. "There was a minor incident a few months back that she witnessed, and we need to get her statement again. It seems, however, that she just... disappeared."

This amused Karen Hartwig to no end, and she burst out laughing, coffee dripping down her chin.

"Disappeared, huh? You're a regular riot, the way you say things." She took another gulp of her coffee, draining the cup, and held it out to him for a refill; Ben didn't hesitate to accommodate her. "She sure did disappear. He disappeared, they all just… poof! Disappeared, just like that."

Karen didn't laugh this time.

Ben brought her back a full cup and sat back down. A pad in hand and pen ready, he asked her if she had any idea where they had gone? Were they still in Cleveland? Were they overseas? Any information she could give him would be of incredibly great help, he said.

After a timid drink of her hot liquid, Karen stared into her cup for a moment, as if looking for life's answers in the strained java beans. After what seemed like an eternity, she looked up at him and gave him a sad smile. She was going to talk… Ben knew it.

"Can I tell you a long story?" she asked. "Well, at least it seems long to me."

Ben nodded. "You can talk to me about anything you like."

A tear came to one eye, and she brushed it away, embarrassed. "Thank you. He's why I drink like this, you know. I never did before… never in my life."

"Who? Who's why?"

Karen gave a half-snort. "Dr. Michael Hall."

Ben's experience told him that now was not the time for questions, not in situations like this. She was bursting at the seams to talk to someone. He was sure that there was more than one bartender in town sick to death of her talking, but he had a fresh ear to lend, and it was ready and waiting. He said nothing, just waited patiently for her to begin when she was ready.

"I started working for Michael just under twelve years ago when he first opened his private practice on Meade Parkway," she began. "I was technically a 'PA,' you know, physician's assistant, but back then we were really no more than nurses who could write prescriptions. Now we are capable of pretty much running the show, as long as a doctor's name is on the sign outside. Anyway, he interviewed me and hired me on the spot. At first, I was the right-hand lady. Over time, my responsibilities grew, and he hired a couple of nurses to do triage and registrations, and the practice did very well."

She took another drink of her coffee; she was really sobering up now. Ben jumped up and grabbed the pot from the small kitchen, rushed it out to her, and refilled her cup before returning it. Sitting back down, he focused his attention back on her intently.

"The affair started almost right away," she said simply. "I fell in love like an idiot would, and Michael made all the promises that men like him make to idiots. Yes, I knew Aneta, his wife. We talked all the time; that's how affairs go, isn't it? Sneaking and pretending and lying, and sneaking some more." She looked up at Ben with that same sad smile, with eyes to match. "I never even felt guilty, because he said he loved me, that their marriage was over long ago, he stayed because of

Shanice, blah, blah, blah."

With a nod of understanding, Ben began to jot in his pad, partially hiding it behind the arm of the loveseat; he didn't want to make her uncomfortable.

Karen continued. "Anyway, years passed. He wanted to wait to leave Aneta until Shanice turned eighteen and graduated. By the beginning of last school year, her junior year, I was beginning to see the light at the end of the tunnel. But, that kid was a little jerk! Always causing some kind of grief, pushing other kids around. Instead of punishing her, or disciplining her, Michael and her mother would talk her out of trouble, or buy her way out. Then there was an incident of assault, and Shanice had to face the music for the first time ever."

"What happened?" he asked, though he already knew.

Karen shrugged, drained her cup, and put it aside, signifying she was done with the coffee. "Well, from what Michael told me, Shanice was pushing some poor girl around at school, some girl she had been targeting for years. One day, she picked the wrong place and time, and another student stepped in. Shanice actually got suspended, which was embarrassing enough for the 'Good Doctor.' He was constantly dancing around to make his personal life look picture perfect, but I knew better."

"Well," Ben said off the cuff, "a daughter getting suspended is hardly a big deal."

Another snort. "It was big enough, but it was the tip of the iceberg. Shanice and a friend of hers ended up jumping the girl in the alley, the one who got her suspended. They drew a bit of blood, I believed and bruised her ribs, but this girl got the best of them in the end. Leaving Shanice with a nasty wound on her face. Because they instigated the attack, both girls were charged, expelled from school, and even had to do a bit of time in juvenile detention. It was the best thing that could have happened in my opinion."

"Um, I'm sorry," Ben said slowly. "I just don't get it. Is this why they moved to Cleveland? And how did this affect you? Because you lost your job? I mean, no offense, Ms. Hartwig, but there are plenty of jobs in your field."

"It's Karen, and let me finish," she told him. "You'll see."

Ben clamped his mouth shut; best not to get pushy.

Karen began to glance around the room, and he knew what she was looking for: a bottle, any bottle. Well, it wasn't going to happen; he got up and refilled her coffee, giving her the last of what was in the pot. With a groan, Karen took the cup and rolled her eyes at him, but offered a slight smile.

"So, anyway," she continued. "When little Shanice caught all this trouble, it spilled over into Michael and Aneta's life like floodwaters. It not only scarred her face but scarred her family as well. They got kicked out of the country club, so-called 'friends' of theirs stopped inviting them to parties, and they became the talk of Greenville among the rich and fortunate. So, while the girl was doing her time, he began to make arrangements to move his practice to Cleveland."

Karen stared down at her coffee, a look of bittersweet shame on her face. "At first, I was crushed; in my eyes, this meant Michael and I were through, of course. I mean, I owned this home my mother left me, and surely he was in the process of hiring new staff that lived in the Cleveland area. What was I to do? It would be nearly a two-hour commute, and I just couldn't do that, neither physically nor financially. I was just crushed.

"But then the miracle happened. One night, when we were rendezvousing in a hotel in downtown Toledo, he told me he wanted me to move and stay with the practice. I could keep the house; he would rent an apartment for me, and Aneta would simply think I relocated for my job. So, I did it, no questions asked. After all, I thought he was 'the one,' the love of my miserable life."

"You're not alone, Karen," Ben said softly. "I understand."

She offered him a thankful smile and went on with her story. "So, here I was in Cleveland, working with him at the new practice, talking smack to Aneta and Shanice, and everyone else working there. All was beautiful and fine. Then, Shanice went and got pregnant by some leather-wearing wannabe biker kid who wore his pants too low and his hair too long."

Ben was shocked. He hadn't expected this revelation at all. An unexpected, embarrassing teen pregnancy explained a lot of things.

"He told me he was going to send her to a home for young, unwed mothers. There, she would have the baby, and it would be put up for adoption." She shook her head at the memory. "There would be no abortion; he wouldn't have it, not as a physician and healer. Instead, like he did with all his daughter's mistakes, he would make it go away. Then, after that, when she came back, he would leave Aneta. Forget waiting for Shanice to turn eighteen. He would give them a lump-sum of money, and he and I would run away to France, get married, and live happily ever after."

Ben looked down at his pad, which had gone forgotten for some time. "But that wasn't what happened, is it?"

Karen chuckled. "Obviously."

"What did happen?"

"Well, on the weekend they were supposed to fly Shanice to this home for unwed mothers. We wrapped up our Friday appointments, and I went home, planning to work on Monday. But when Monday came, and I went to work, there was a sign hanging on the entrance that read: 'Practice is permanently closed. Current patients have been referred. We apologize for any inconvenience, and thank you for your patronage.' I tried to call him. His cell was turned off, the business phone was disconnected, and so was his home phone. When I went to their home, it had been completely cleaned out, bare as a skeleton picked clean. A For Sale sign was in the front yard, so I called the realtor. She informed me that Dr. Hall had relocated, and she would handle the sale through escrow if I were interested in the property. She would give me no forwarding numbers or address.

"So, like any modern human would do, I search my brains out and drink vodka ever since. Like you said, he disappeared. However, I did run into one of the nurses from the Cleveland practice right after speaking to the realtor; funny, I ran into her at a liquor store. Anyway, she told me she had been one to help clean the offices out, and she had found a flyer for a girls' home in Switzerland in Michael's desk drawer."

Ben struggled to control himself, to keep from sitting forward eagerly. "The family went to Switzerland?"

Karen shrugged and set down her now-cold coffee. "I called the home, but they had no Shanice Hall in residence, nor did they know of or have any working relationship with Dr. Michael Hall. I know what he did, though."

"What did he do, Karen?" Ben asked gently.

"What any loving, massively-enabling parent would do," she replied with a bitter smile. "He moved them away, out of the country, and changed their identities. Likely, Shanice was in that home, but I doubt very highly that her name is Shanice anymore. She would have that baby around November or December, but my dates are likely wrong." She turned to him and leaned forward, her elbows resting on her knees, which poked out from under the robe. "I don't think he ended up putting her in that home anyway. I think once he decided to 'start over fresh,' without me, they hid, and likely they are going to claim the baby as their own. You know why I drink, don't you, Officer?"

"Detective," Ben corrected. He thought he knew, but he bit. "Why, Karen? Please call me Ben."

"Ben, I drink because it is more than painfully clear that Michael Hall took me for a ride emotionally for the entirety of our relationship. Every word was a lie, every promise was baloney. I hate that I didn't see it. I can see right through a drug addict who is lying for a prescription, but I couldn't see through him."

He felt terrible for her. "Karen, love is blind."

A tear rolled down her cheek. "In my case, it's blind, mute, deaf, and stupid, too."

Ben decided right then and there he wasn't going to write anything down until he left. He also had a pretty good feeling that Shanice Hall wouldn't be found, at least not any time soon. He tucked his pad and pen into his suit coat with a sigh.

"I'm sorry," he said. "But as long as you're breathing, there is hope."

"Yeah," she mumbled. "Hope."

"If I may, I'd like to ask you just one question, and then I'll let you be to do whatever you need to do. Is that okay?"

She nodded and began to look around for stray booze bottles again.

"During the time the Toledo practice was open, particularly last fall, did any type of gas, such as sleeping gas or other similar anesthesia, ever come up short at the practice?"

The question immediately got her attention, and she stopped dead, her mind obviously racing. "You know, it happened a few times, and not just last fall. Small tanks, I think three of them total, were stolen from the offices and the paper chain was falsified. As a matter of fact, a young nurse was fired over it. I can't remember her name, but I told Michael she hadn't done it. I knew it was Shanice; that girl loved to get high on whatever she could get her hands on."

The answer satisfied Ben so much that he decided to give Karen Hartwig a leg up.

"Get dressed, Karen," he told her as he rose to his feet. "Let's get you to the liquor store. Maybe tomorrow you can sober up, but I can't leave you like this, not after all I've dredged up."

R.W.K. Clark

CHAPTER 17

Mavis sat on the patio in the shade. She was home alone, and since her father and mother had forbidden her from going anywhere unaccompanied due to the issues with Candy Wilkes, she found herself spending more and more time outside, in the back, with Feisty. Matt always slept during morning hours, and she was missing him, anxious for his afternoon visit.

Regardless of his night-shift job, Matt always made sure to drop off her "breakfast" while she slept, leaving it in a cooler outside her bedroom window on his way home from work. He always put a little note inside for her; today it had said he was thinking of her, loved her, and to stay home. Well, he'd be happy to know she was doing as he asked.

There hadn't been any obvious signs of Candy since her family got the restraining order. The girl had left no more morbid gifts for her or her family to find, and no more outwardly aggressive phone calls. At least three times a day, Mavis got "restricted" calls on her cell, which meant the caller was blocking the number from which they were calling. But never a word was ever spoken; the caller simply sat and listened to her, obviously getting off on being a pain in the rear.

The truth was, Mavis wasn't the slightest bit worried about the girl, or what the girl would do to her. Yes, she was a bit concerned about Matt's safety. What if Candy had truly gone off the deep end and one day really tried to hurt him, or worse yet, got the job done? She didn't think it would happen, but you never could tell.

What Mavis was really worried about was what she might do to Candy.

She and Matt were going to great lengths to control her feasting "outbursts." He supplied her with fresh flesh, she went through atrocious amounts of vapor rub and perfume on a daily basis, and she kept her distance from places with a lot of people, which might pique her appetite if she smelled their sweat or skin. She stayed home more than ever in her life, doing so even before all this trouble began, and everything she did, she did with real concern for the safety of others. It helped that she knew what she was and had come to understand what she was capable of, and Matthew was a huge part of that. Most of all, she wanted her parents kept in blissful oblivion regarding her condition. If Candy, who had no idea that Mavis was a zombie, got hold of her at the wrong place and time, there was no telling what the outcome could be, but she knew it would be terrible. When she went into that mode, that state that drove her to kill and eat, she had absolutely no control. It would kill her parents if this came out, and she simply could not let herself destroy them in that way.

The truth was, she hadn't spoken to anyone about

this fear. Not Kim, not Matt, no one. Last night she had dreamed of eating Candy Wilkes. The dream had been so real she could taste flesh and blood. She was enjoying every second of it, making the biggest mess of the girl's body she could, just because it felt so good to do it. When she woke that morning, she had been so shaken with temptation she was nearly able to justify committing the act. It took her two hours to get her wits about her and her own mind right.

Today, Matt would be there around four in the afternoon. Mavis promised herself that she would tell him her feelings then. Maybe he could soothe her, or suggest a solution that would appease her desires. But the truth was, she hated the girl for many reasons, the greatest being what she was doing to her family right now. Forget the silly assault from last year; that was nothing compared to the worry and grief she saw on the faces of her parents and Matthew on a daily basis. The girl deserved to become a great big snack.

Picking up her cell off the patio table, she thought about calling Kim. Her best friend had gotten extremely serious with Shawn Maher over the last months, and they were even discussing marriage after graduation. Mavis thought it was a wonderful idea; they were a perfect couple, she had to admit, just like her and Matt.

After pondering whether or not she should call, Mavis decided it would be best. She was feeling a bit depressed, and it didn't help that she and Kim were growing apart as they grew up. Mavis supposed that was the reality of life, but it didn't make it hurt any less. In her mind, the way to keep a friendship alive was by actively taking steps to do just that. She found Kim's name in her contacts and tapped it; soon, the phone was ringing.

"Hey, girl! What's up?" The voice of her best friend made her smile immediately.

At first, the conversation was light. Kim was deep cleaning her room at her mother's insistence because the woman had found a plate under her bed with month-old chicken bones on it. She had plans with Shawn for the weekend, but he was busy helping his father on his uncle's farm for the next two days. The girls made plans to hang out at Donnelly Park and have a picnic the next afternoon, which made Mavis very happy. It was then that the tone of the conversation changed.

"Mav, what's wrong?" Kim suddenly asked. "Don't try to lie to me, because I'll know."

As soon as she opened her mouth to answer, all of her grief, loneliness, and anger at Candy Wilkes came gushing out. She cried at first, then expressed her fear. Next, her anger came out in torrents, and she told Kim how badly she wanted to sink her teeth into the girl's neck and tear out her jugular. Her tirade went on for ten minutes, and just like a best friend should, Kim listened with love and compassion, in silence.

When finally her rant passed, Mavis lay back on the patio recliner, spent from the emotion, and tried to calm herself and her breathing. It was then that Kim took the wheel. It was no surprise that the girl who had been her best friend nearly her entire life knew just how to talk to her, just what to say to get her back into her right mind. Mavis found herself wishing she had called her earlier.

"Mavis, I listened to you, now it's your turn to listen," she began. "I want you to think about Candy for a minute… really think about her as a person. I know that she has done, and is doing, some pretty unsavory, scandalous crap, but just consider what it must be like to be her."

Mavis listened intently to what her friend was saying, mostly because it was the same thing she would be telling Kim if the tables were turned.

Kim continued. "She's been a follower all of her life, we know this by her choice of friends. Her mother and father are religious fanatics. When she got into trouble with the assault, instead of letting her adjust to Shanice's absence and make new friends, they pulled her out of school. They stopped all socialization, isolated her, and made her dress funny. They took away her makeup! She doesn't even know who she is! The last time she did, she was Shanice's lackey. She can't even find herself.

"The cops are all over her because of the murders, which we won't even discuss, and you know why. She's lonely, scared, and angry. Instead of making her into a Candy on Rye with Mayo, why not consider befriending her, if and when this all passes and blows over? I mean, hopefully, she doesn't go to prison for something she didn't do, but whatever happens, you have the choice to either be just like she is now or try to make it better. Yes, she has a bad heart right now, and maybe she deserves prison for reasons we'll never know. But Mavis, I swear, you gotta stop feeling sorry for yourself over this. While it isn't your direct fault, it is your doing."

With that being said, Kim went silent and waited for her friend to respond. Mavis knew that Kim was bracing herself, frightened of how her best pal was going to respond. But she shouldn't have worried; Mavis knew every word spoken was true.

"You're right," she replied simply, wiping her tears as she spoke. "I feel crappy, almost like a milder version of Shanice herself. I don't want her to get into trouble, but it seems like she is trying to like she's forcing it to happen for the killings. Just think about the doll she sent."

Kim didn't hesitate to respond. "If you lived her life, prison might sound good to you, too."

Mavis took a deep breath and put her chin up. "This is why I love you, you know. What would I do without you?"

Kim snorted. "You'd probably eat the poor girl, that's what. Now go inside, wash your face, comb your hair, and put some makeup on so you can see Matt looking like a princess instead of a beaten down pauper. I'll see you two tomorrow, all right?"

"Absolutely."

"I love you, ya know." Kim suddenly said.

Mavis smiled. "I love you, too."

CHAPTER 18

"Can I help you, sir?"

Ben Gordon stood at the main reception desk at Heavenly Haven Convalescence Center, a home for the aged and dying. The place smelled horrible, diapers and pureed food, but visually it appeared to be immaculate. Everywhere he looked he saw smiling nurses and blank elderly faces. Flowers filled vases on nearly every table available, and a small group of residents who used wheelchairs engaged in a game of cards. All were staring at him, hoping against hope that he was there to visit one of them.

"Yes, ma'am," he replied with his most charming smile. "I'm Detective Ben Gordon of the Greenville PD. Do you have an aide by the name of Jessica Reynolds in your employ?"

The woman at the desk lost her smile the way one might lose their gas cap at the station when in a hurry. "Um, we do… is there a problem that perhaps I could help you with?"

"No, ma'am, no problem at all." Ben let his charming smile grow. "Ms. Reynolds has done nothing wrong. I'm working on an old case, and she was a witness at the time. I just need to verify some information before we take the case to trial, that's all."

The woman's smile came back like gangbusters. "Sure, I can page her for you. I believe she's on the Alzheimer's Unit today so it might take her a minute to get up here. It's a secure unit, there are policies for entrance and exit. If you'd like to have a seat, I'll give her a page for you."

"Thank you very much."

Ben turned and gave a friendly smile to the card players, all of whom turned away in disappointment and went back to their game. Next to the double automatic glass doors which he had entered through was a row of chairs, each with a table separating them. Various magazines were stacked neatly on the tables, and he wondered momentarily how old the magazines were.

"Only one way to find out," he mumbled to himself.

He took the first seat and began to sort through the closest stack. An issue of sports magazine from 2005 was the first thing of interest he found, so he began to flip through it disinterestedly, glancing up on occasion to see if anyone was approaching him. After ten minutes, he got engrossed in an article about a football player, who happened to be "Sportsperson of the Year."

Ben lost track of time as he read, and by the time he finished the article, he had been waiting for a half-hour. Putting down the magazine, he stood to go back to the reception desk and remind them of his presence. Right at that moment, he saw a woman of about twenty-seven approaching him with a smile. She had blond, shoulder-length curly hair, a sweet face, and attractive figure, and she wore a black scrub outfit with little mouse appliques all over it. He stopped and flashed his famous smile.

"Are you Jessica, by chance?"

The girl nodded and returned his smile, but he could tell by the look in her eyes that she was nervous about his visit. He held out his hand pleasantly, and when she reached him, she took it and shook it briefly before quickly pulling it away and tucking it safely in her scrub shirt pocket.

"Um, yes, I am." She glanced around the common area nervously but maintained her smile. "How can I help you, Detective…?"

"Gordon," he stated. "But please, call me Ben. Is there somewhere we could talk privately? I just have some questions about an old case I'm working on. Don't worry; you're safe."

The girl breathed a sigh of relief, and her face softened dramatically. "Follow me; there's a family meeting room over here for hospice interviews that isn't being used. Would you like something to drink?"

"No, thank you. Just had coffee."

A couple of minutes later, they were seated at a long rectangular table in the most uncomfortable, stiff vinyl chairs that Ben had ever had the displeasure of sitting in. Nothing like talking about the death of a loved one while sitting bolt upright with a backache, he thought.

"How can I help you?" Jessica asked.

He cleared his throat and pulled out his pad and pen. "Well, I'm investigating an incident involving the daughter of one of your past employers, a Dr. Michael Hall?"

Fear came over her face again. "Listen, sir. Dr. Hall fired me for something I didn't do. No charges were pressed because the allegations couldn't be proven. I lost my nursing license, and now I have to change beds and diapers for a living. I have more than paid for the trouble that incident caused."

Ben put down his pad and pen, put his elbows on the table, and leaned toward her, making sure she could see his smile clearly. "Jessica, I believe you. I suspect another was responsible for the crime. I just need details as to what substances were stolen, if you know any possible details, and if you can remember approximate dates."

Now she relaxed visibly once again. "I'd be glad to help, in that case. Are you ready to write?"

Snatching up his pen, Ben said, "Shoot."

"It was his daughter, Shanice," Jessica began. "First, I caught her stealing samples of Valium out of the drug closet. She cornered me, and believe me when I say she was a mean one, scary even. She threatened to have me fired if I didn't falsify the records, so I did, and of that I was guilty. But it didn't stop there. Once she knew she had me, the game continued, with everything from pain pills to anesthetic gases. Once, when she thought we were pals or something, she joked how she and her friends could party hard thanks to me."

"What was the last thing she took, and the approximate date, if you can remember?"

"Let's see…" Her eyes went to the ceiling in thought. "If I remember correctly, the last thing was nitrous, I believe. It wasn't much, just a couple smaller canisters, but I remember scolding her. I was worried the kids playing with it would overdo it. It's safe when used in correct dosages; doesn't knock you out, just makes you sort of… stop caring… happy. But too much and it could be lights out."

Ben scribbled away. "Why didn't you say something to her father right away, when it first began?"

"That girl had Dr. Hall wrapped around her finger. Don't get me wrong, he knew how she was, what she was capable of, but he was so concerned with his own image that he would have done anything to anyone to keep his sparkling public appearance. Her threat to me wasn't empty, and he would have put me through the wringer if I had tried to make waves."

"How did your firing come about?"

She gave a slight shrug as if trying to convince herself that none of it mattered anymore, though the sting was still fresh. "I'm not sure… I think he must have caught her with some of the pills because that was all he ever asked me about; the gas never came up. Anyway, when I tried to tell him the truth, he fired me on the spot and told me that if I tried to fight him, he would take legal action. My signatures were on the inventory sheets; it was a no-win situation."

Ben felt disgusted; no wonder Shanice Hall was such a vile human being. Her father had raised her that way with his own behavior and the covering he did for hers.

The girl before him had suffered terribly for simply trying to keep her job.

"I'm sorry this happened to you."

The girl shrugged again. "What's done is done. Is there anything else? I still have two sets of rounds, plus lunch to serve."

"No, this is perfect," he replied, standing to shake her hand once again. "Thank you for your time, and I hope things find their way in your favor once again."

"Thanks."

They left the room together, and she walked away without looking back. He watched her, his heart aching for the injustice she had suffered, even though she had chosen the wrong course of action, to begin with. It seemed that the Hall family, in general, were nothing but a bunch of bullies who constantly had their own image and appearance in mind. They strove to protect them at any cost, no matter who got hurt along the way.

Regardless, Ben now had a much clearer picture of how Candy might have been able to overcome an entire gymnasium full of adults and nearly-grown teens. It would have been easy, lickety-split, with the use of something like laughing gas. Now it was time to get a search warrant for the Wilkes home. It would be interesting to see if any evidence of the dope heists lingered there.

CHAPTER 19

"It's such a beautiful day, I say we put the top down on my car and take it to Donnelly Park for our picnic." Mavis was in an especially good mood, excited to spend time with both Kim and Matt. "Then, afterward, we can go for a cruise, turn up the music, and enjoy the weather; what do you think?"

Matt winked at her as he placed several sodas in a small cooler with ice. "I can drive, right?"

Mavis rolled her eyes. "Hmmm... I should have known. Of course."

"Okay, guys, the food is packed." Kim Coleman took the large picnic basket off the kitchen table and got a firm grip on it with both hands. "It feels like I got everything. At least, it's definitely heavy enough that I'm convincing myself of that."

"But do we have everything?" Mavis knew that, while Kim had the best of intentions, the slightly flighty girl almost always forgot something important when they did things like this together. The last time they had a picnic they had taken potato salad, but she had forgotten to pack any utensils to eat it with.

Kim thought about it. "I guess I'd better double

check."

She put the basket back on the table, opened it up, and started to take inventory. "Let's see… three double-stacked hoagies, six mini bags of potato chips, a container of cold baked beans, paper plates, napkins, three complete sets of plastic utensils… see? I remembered those this time! Um… Matt's got the soda pop, and Mavis has the music and blanket. I think we're good."

"What about mayo and mustard?" Mavis asked, knowing that the sandwiches would be horribly dry without them.

Matt opened the fridge without missing a beat. "I'll get them. They'll need to go into the cooler anyway. Pickles, anyone?"

Mavis nodded. "Better grab them."

In ten minutes' time, the trio had the little car packed, and they were soon tooling the short distance to Donnelly Park. The sun was shining, the temperature was just right, and there was a slight warm breeze when the car wasn't moving down the road; it couldn't have been a better day. The kids weren't at all surprised when they arrived and saw tons of other people milling around, playing frisbee golf, strolling, or just lounging in the sun.

"I should have brought Feisty," Mavis thought aloud. "He would have loved this."

Matt shook his head. "There are too many other dogs, and they all seem to be bigger than he is. Besides, Feisty isn't used to playing with other pooches. It was best to leave him."

Though the park was packed, they easily found a perfect spot for the blanket. It was right along the edge of the wooded area that surrounded the large picnic and barbecuing area, and it was a fair enough distance from other park visitors that they would be able to enjoy each other's company without interruption.

Matt backed the car into a nearby spot, and the three of them proceeded to set up their midday meal. The first thing Mavis did was put music on her smartphone and plug it into her portable speaker deck, making sure the volume wasn't so loud that it bothered anyone nearby. It was pretty heavy music, and she had quickly learned that it didn't appeal to everyone's taste when she started listening to it several months ago.

"I hope you plan on providing a bit more variety," Kim said almost immediately; she was still a fan of the more "poppy" genre, and bands with Heavy Metal names made her cringe.

Mavis smiled as she turned to lay out the blanket. "Of course. My playlist is still pretty versatile, even if I don't listen to some of it at all anymore."

"Ugh," Kim muttered with a roll of her eyes. "Good."

Soon, the three of them were settled down comfortably on the blanket, opening their sandwiches and chips. It didn't take them long to dig in, their conversation light and cheerful between bites. Kim made it a point to catch up Matt and Mavis on how things were going with her and Shawn, which seemed to be wonderful. The girl was very excited about the prospect of marrying him after graduation. Shawn planned to join the Marine Corps, a decision he had recently made. He wanted to learn some technical trade that they would teach him, but Kim couldn't exactly remember what it was specifically. She voiced nervousness about him opting for the military, but she was so starry-eyed over the young man that Mavis knew she would do anything for him, going anywhere he wanted to go.

After an hour, it was obvious that all three of them were purposefully avoiding any conversation about zombies or girls with vendettas, and this made Mavis a bit uncomfortable. As close as she was to both Kim and Matt, she felt like it should be at least briefly discussed. After all, they were with her to hang out and to see to it that nothing happened to her, at least, according to her parents' recent restrictions for her safety.

But she also didn't want to continue to beat a dead horse and wear out her best companions. She tried her best to keep thoughts of Candy and all that was related to her own "crimes" out of the conversation and her mind. The result ended up being a slightly awkward lull in the conversation right at the end of their meal, but as usual, Matt saved the day.

"Kim, I thought you said you brought everything," he said suddenly with a gleam in his eye.

The girl looked up at him, a piece of deli turkey hanging half out of her mouth and a bit of mayo on her upper lip. "What? What did I forget?"

Matt didn't miss a beat. "Um… dessert? The individual chocolate pies that I set on the table next to the basket for you to pack."

"Oh, gosh!" Kim dramatically tossed the last of her sandwich on her plate and flung herself back onto the blanket. "Not the chocolate pies, of all things!"

If anything gave Kim a shot to the heart, it would be the lack of dessert. Matt was playful, and her reaction entertained him to no end. His plate was empty, so he took a chug of his soda, wiped his mouth, and stood up.

"Never fear, Kim my dear," he teased. "Mav, I'm going to run to the house and grab the pies. Is the back door open?"

Mavis laughed and nodded, giving him a wink. "Yeah. You might wanna grab my sunscreen; I'm feeling a little flaky."

"You are flaky."

Matt bent down and planted a kiss on her cheek while Kim sat up to finish her food.

That was when it happened.

Just as Matt stood back up to go to the car, a slight zinging sound whizzed by Mavis' head. Confused, she began to look around, but then she heard another, this one briefer. Then another, which was followed by a loud "ping"!

"Ouch! What the?" Matt grabbed at his leg, a pained look coming over his face. When he pulled his hand away from his outer left thigh, near the knee, Mavis saw blood flowering and blooming through the denim of his holey jeans like a bright poppy that was growing before her very eyes.

Kim screamed, and her hand went up to her mouth, her eyes wide. People were turning to look, and Mavis began to dart her eyes madly around her surroundings. Subconsciously, she took note of most everyone, even a shadow of a figure just inside the wooded area, who appeared to be running away at a very fast pace, darting through the trees and out of sight.

"Somebody shot me!" Matt yelled.

Mavis jumped up. "Oh, my! Is it a bullet?"

Matt sat down hard on the blanket, more out of shock than pain. "I don't think so; it doesn't hurt like I would think a bullet would." With shaking hands, he grabbed at the hole in the knee of his jeans and ripped upward, exposing the wound. A tiny hole in his thigh was leaking just enough blood to look bad, but Mavis knew right away that it was more than likely a pellet or BB.

"Okay, now I'm pissed!"

She could smell his blood suddenly, and her head began to swim. But trusty Matt saw the change come over her face right away. Thinking fast, he scrambled away from her on his hands and knees, ignoring the pain, until he was about fifteen feet from her.

"Kim, get her to the car and get her vapor rub on," he shouted, but Kim was staring at him, stuck and stunned. Mavis had a blank look on her face, just staring at his leg, her mouth wide open.

"Kim, now!"

She snapped out of it then and grabbed Mavis by the

arm, practically dragging her to the car. At first, Mavis fought her a bit, but once she jerked her eyes off Matt to turn her attention on to her friend, she too snapped out of it. Panicked by her own thoughts, she bolted to the car as fast as she could, with Kim stumbling behind her.

Mavis opened the passenger door and practically fell into the front seat. With a single flip of her hand, she opened the glove box. The small jar of vapor rub fell out onto the floor. She couldn't get it under her nose fast enough. After a few deep inhalations, all she could smell was the potent menthol aroma, and she began to calm down.

When her mind was completely clear, she looked around for Kim. The girl was bent over slightly at the back of the car, staring at something. Mavis got out and went to see what she was doing. As she did, she saw that Matt had stood and was making his way back to the blanket with a limp.

"What is it, Kim?" Her friend looked up at her, fear in her eyes, and started to back away. "No! I'm fine! I got to the vapor rub... it's cool!"

Kim stopped, relieved, then pointed to the rear of the small white car. "Look, Mav. They shot your taillight, too."

Mavis looked at the red lens cover to see a small hole, which had branched out, cracking in several directions all around the initial puncture. It pissed her off, but she was glad. Certainly, the projectile would be in there somewhere.

In a voice icy with anger, Mavis said, "Let's get our stuff together. I'm going to the cops right now. Someone was in the woods almost right behind us, and they took off running. I didn't see who it was, but I have my suspicions."

By the time they turned to go to Matt, he was already coming down the hill, limping and livid with anger. The girls went to gather up their things, and then they shoved them haphazardly into the trunk. Mavis slammed it shut while Matt and Kim got into the car.

"I'm driving," she said in a tone that was not to be argued with.

As they pulled out of the park, Mavis' jaw was set, and she was so angry she couldn't even speak. Both Matt and Kim remained quiet for a bit, both to let her process and to see where she was going. Soon, it was obvious they were going to Greenville Medical Center.

Mavis spoke before they could ask. "We'll go to the ER, then we're going to see that cop. This is going to stop, Matt. I saw someone running. I didn't get a clear view, but if it was an accident, why did they run? The person was right behind us in the woods. They were so close they could hear our conversation! I'm so pissed, and I've had enough of this crap!"

Pulling into a parking space in the Emergency Room lot, she shut off the ignition and pulled up the e-brake. As she was getting out of the car, Matt put his hand on her arm and stopped her. Mavis whirled her head to look at him, fire in her eyes.

"What?"

He paused, giving her a chance to get control of herself, his eyes telling her that was what she needed to do. After she took several deep breaths, she calmly looked at him. There was no need to say anything; she just waited for him to speak.

"While you and Kim were at the car, a few other people ran over to see what happened," Matt said in a low voice. "Two of them told me they saw someone with a red ball cap sitting in the bushes, but they didn't think anything of it until I screamed. One of them saw the person running away too."

Mavis didn't allow her friends to see the anger she felt; it would get her nowhere to let her emotions run the show. "Let's go inside and deal with your leg. I'll call Detective Gordon while we're here."

As they made their way into the emergency area, Mavis was already punching up the detective's number, fortunately having his card in her purse. She made a decision right then to put it as a permanent contact. It infuriated her to no end that she had to do it at all.

R.W.K. Clark

CHAPTER 20

Ben Gordon left Greenville Medical Center with rage pumping through his veins, his step purposeful and his eyes hard as steel. He took no notice of anyone or anything around him; his focus was on getting to his car and serving the Wilkes family with a search warrant. He had been in the process of obtaining when he received the call from Mavis Harvey telling him that Matthew Morgan had been shot in the leg with a pellet gun, as had her car.

He reached his vehicle and got inside, then proceeded to call for a single car to assist him in search of the Wilkes home. He directed the officers to meet him at their address, then he pulled out of the lot and started for the freeway. During the drive, he turned things over in his mind, pondering and dwelling on the story the three kids had just told him.

No one had seen Candy Wilkes, at least, not enough to identify her directly. There was no sure way of knowing if it was her in the woods wielding that pellet gun, but everyone had their suspicions, and for a good reason. The warrant was granting them permission to search for signs of stolen medications or laughing gas canisters, or anything else that could tie the girl to drugs taken from Dr. Hall's practice. If they happened to find a pellet gun, well, they couldn't be blamed for hauling her in after the day's incidents.

Ben sped all the way to the Wilkes residence, arriving to see that the squad he had requested was already there, waiting for him a couple of houses up. He parked directly in front of the residence and gave the place a good, hard look. It appeared to be completely quiet; even the drapes were drawn, shutting out the beauty of the day. It seemed that the Wilkeses weren't home; what a coincidence.

Pulling away from the curb, he drove up alongside the squad car and rolled down the passenger window; the driver of the squad did the same with his.

"It looks to me like they're not in," he said, leaning over the passenger seat. "I'm compelled to conduct this search today, so let's go get some coffee and come back. They'll be home."

The cop nodded, and both cars took off. They went to Zippy Stop, a convenience store about a half-mile from the Wilkes home. There, Ben picked up the tab for three large black coffees and a variety box of donuts. The men then returned to Candy's house, where they parked up the block, keeping the place in full view so they could see when the occupants returned. It didn't take long; Ben got in a single bite of donut and two drinks of coffee when a forest green sedan approached them and pulled into the Wilkes driveway. Ben looked over at the squad car and gave the men a single nod, then pulled out and parked in front of the house himself. The squad followed suit and parked behind him, blocking the driveway.

"Mr. and Mrs. Wilkes!"

Ben was out of his car in a flash, warrant in hand and a smile on his face. Mrs. Wilkes was walking just behind a short, balding man of about forty, who Ben could only guess was her husband. Candy was just getting out of the back seat and closing the door. As soon as she saw him her face fell, and he could swear she turned white.

She was wearing knee-length denim shorts, a light long-sleeved t-shirt, and a red ball cap.

The family all stood looking at him, and after a moment, Mr. Wilkes spoke. "Yes, I'm Mr. Wilkes. Can I help you?"

As Ben and the two uniformed officers approached, he heard Mrs. Wilkes say, "Dear, this is the detective I have been telling you about." He noticed she was glancing, with confusion, at the two in uniform. Candy looked as if she wanted to throw up. Yeah, I bet you're just sick, he thought.

"Mr. Wilkes, I'm Detective Ben Gordon with the Greenville Police," he began. "These men here are Officers Miller and Harris of the same." He handed Candy's father the folded piece of paper he held in his hand. "We are here to serve you with a signed court order permitting us to search your property, sir."

The man looked stunned. He opened the paperwork and scanned it with his eyes. "What's this all about?

What is it that you're looking for?"

The man went to the porch and unlocked the house, at which point the two officers entered and began to search. Mr. and Mrs. Wilkes, along with Candy and Ben, stood on the front porch so they could all keep an eye on things and talk at the same time. Candy was the one who seemed nervous, though Mrs. Wilkes voiced concern about her home being torn up; Ben reassured her that the officers would exercise care during the process.

"Could you tell me where you and your family have been today, sir?" Ben asked.

The man didn't hesitate with his answer. "Yes, we had a family reunion at my brother's house from ten this morning until just under an hour ago."

"Where does your brother live?"

Mr. Wilkes looked like he was getting perturbed, but being a church-going man, he wouldn't argue, Ben knew.

"He lives in Greenville, on Martin's Circle. Three-twenty-five, to be exact." He shifted his weight from one foot to the other and crossed his arms over his chest. "What does this have to do with searching my home? In fact, why are you searching my home?"

Ben gave him a sympathetic smile; the poor guy just didn't have a clue about the things his daughter had been up to during the prior school year. "We believe your daughter might be in possession of items related to some thefts that took place at a medical practice last fall."

Candy turned pale, and her eyes went directly to the ground.

"There's nothing in the daughter's room, sir."

The two officers stood in the living room now, waiting for their next set of instructions, which Ben was nearly ready to give.

"We'll need access to your garage and car also, sir," he said to Mr. Wilkes.

The man looked defeated, glared at his daughter, and gave a long sigh. "Of course, Officers. Right, this way."

As the two patrolmen followed Mr. Wilkes around to the garage, Ben directed his gaze at Candy, who pretended not to notice. "So, Candy, what did you do at the family reunion?"

The girl shrugged and pushed a small rock around with her sandaled foot.

"The children played games and watched movies in the downstairs rec area while the adults had a croquet tournament," Mrs. Wilkes answered. "Isn't that right, Candy?" There was a sharp tone to her voice, and when the girl didn't answer her, she repeated the question, this time through clenched teeth.

Finally, Candy replied, "Yes… mostly. Me and Jimmy Lou and a couple of the little kids might have gotten bored and took a walk."

Like a flash, Mrs. Wilkes reached out and grabbed her daughter's arm, jerking her hard and making the girl look her in the eye. "You left the house after you were strictly forbidden?"

"Only for a little bit! Maybe a half-hour…" She jerked her arm back and rubbed the spot where her mother had grabbed her.

"Where did you go, young lady?"

Candy took a step back; she looked afraid, and Ben didn't blame her. The girl was in big trouble. She'd been up to no good, someone had gotten hurt as a result, and they both knew it. Well, her parents were about to find out, too.

"Just to Donnelly to push the kids on the swings at the playground," she muttered. "Then we went right back, I swear."

Ben Gordon smiled, shook his head, and clucked his tongue. Right then, Officer Miller rounded the corner with a silver canister in his grasp, which he held onto with a gloved hand. He held the dust-covered item up as best he could with one hand, which told Gordon that the canister was likely empty. Officer Harris and Mr. Wilkes, who was now beet-red, appeared around the corner behind him.

"We found a medical anesthetic canister of what is labeled as Nitrous Oxide," Miller said, giving Candy a brief glance. "I don't believe there is anything in it, sir."

"Doesn't matter," Ben replied. "It's evidence. Now the car; pay special attention to the trunk, please."

Mr. Wilkes looked as though he wanted to pass out, but he made it to the vehicle and unlocked the trunk while his wife began to shake from her anger. "Candy, what were you doing with a Nitrous Oxide container?"

The girl said nothing.

In less than ten seconds, Officer Harris stepped out from behind the car and held up what appeared to be a rifle. "Gordon, it's a .177 caliber air rifle, sir… and a box of pellets, which has been opened."

"Evidence it up, and collect the red ball cap," Ben turned to Candy. "What happened at Donnelly Park today? What did you do?"

Candy said nothing; she simply stared at the ground.

"Oh, please, help us with this child," Mrs. Wilkes said, directing her words toward the sky. "Detective, what has she done?"

Ben took his handcuffs off his belt and took Candy gently by the arm. She tried to pull away, but her mother grabbed her and held her in place. Ben read the girl her rights as he cuffed her, then Miller retrieved the girl to take her to the squad car.

"I'll need my cuffs back, Miller."

With a nod, the officer led her off. Mr. Wilkes yelled at his wife, telling her he was going to follow the girl to the detention center and get their attorney to meet him. Ben stayed to speak with the mother, who was simply enraged.

"I don't know what she's done, but I am so sorry," she said. "Whatever punishment she gets, I hope it fits the crime. I'm at my wits' end."

Ben filled her in. "Today, the boyfriend of Mavis Harvey was shot in the leg with a pellet gun while picnicking with Mavis and her best friend at Donnelly Park. He had to have the pellet dug out of his thigh. Mavis' taillight was also shot out, and the projectiles will match that gun, I'm sure."

"I'm afraid they will. That gun has been in the cellar for years," Mrs. Wilkes said sadly. "Must have dug it out and put it in the car last night. She's been stalking this girl like a hound dog!"

"It appears that way." Ben paused so she could process everything, then continued. "Candy is looking at many charges, including theft and possession of the canister if it proves to be the one that was stolen. I suggest you say nothing more to me without your attorney present, ma'am."

With that, he told her goodbye and started for his car, but before he got too far, Mrs. Wilkes yelled, "Detective Gordon?"

He turned to her. "Yes, ma'am?"

"I love my daughter." A tear rolled down her cheek. "But I don't know where we went wrong. I just don't know, and I'm so sorry."

"I know, ma'am."

As Ben pulled away from the curb, he glanced in the rearview mirror and saw Mrs. Wilkes standing on the porch staring after him. He felt sorry for her, and he felt even worse regarding the future of her confused daughter. Who knew how these things happened, especially when parents really loved their kids and did their best to raise them right?

In his heart, he was starting to believe that incarceration, for any length of time, was the thing that was going to help Candace Wilkes. If it turned out she was involved in the murders, she was going to have a lifetime to get the help she needed. It was a sad story indeed.

It was time to head to the detention center and do some interrogating.

R.W.K. Clark

.

CHAPTER 21

Sitting in the bedroom with no music or television, just processing the horrible events that put an end to what started out to be a perfect day was the one thing Mavis and Kim could think of to do. Kim was on the floor in the beanbag chair, staring straight ahead, replaying the way Matt's blood blossomed through his thin jeans over and over in her mind. It might not have been especially deadly or graphic, but for someone with her weak stomach, it was hard to unsee.

Mavis, on the other hand, lay on her bed staring at the ceiling. She, too, was silent, but she wasn't thinking about Matt's blood, or even her broken taillight, which had to be completely removed by police when they were looking for the stray pellet. Her car was now in the driveway with no driver-side taillight, Matt was at home sleeping off a pain pill the doctor gave him at the ER, and Mavis was lying there thinking about serious, intentional murder.

At the hospital, the doctor had easily dug a tiny pellet out of Matt's leg, put a butterfly stitch over the wound for nothing more than effect, gave him a pill, then allowed Detective Gordon to have a word with them. He gave Matt an antibiotic prescription and sent the kids on their way. The detective had listened to their story, and though he encouraged them to keep an open mind, that maybe Candy Wilkes hadn't been the shooter, she could tell that he, too, thought she was. When he had left the hospital room, the look on his face and his purposeful walk said it all.

The ride to Matt's house had been quiet... too quiet. Mavis had crazy thoughts running through her head due to his silence. What if he realized that he didn't need the hassle or drama of dating a zombie? What if the reality of her wanting to eat him when he was bleeding had hit him hard, and he was actually afraid of her? Once she had gotten him home, and they had given Mrs. Morgan a partial-truth story about what had happened, and they left, she talked to Kim briefly on the way to the Harvey house about her concerns. Kim told her she was nuts, and that Matt was just buzzing from the pain pill, and that she had other things to worry about, like Candy actually killing him. Mavis was furious and sick to her stomach over the entire thing.

Now, the girls sat in the room, mentally and emotionally worn out from the entire incident, and Mavis' thoughts had progressively gone from bad to worse. She was thinking about actually getting rid of Candy Wilkes, eating her to the bone and then giving the bones to old man Hardy's dog down at the junkyard. After all, if the cops weren't going to be able to stop all of the girl's shenanigans, somebody had to do it. Mavis seriously thought she was the only one who could, not to mention the fact that she knew the entire mess was her fault, and therefore, her responsibility.

An hour ago, Detective Gordon had called Mavis' cell phone to tell her that Candy had been arrested and was facing multiple charges, including being charged for shooting Matt. As it turned out, they found a pellet gun in her possession that should not have been there, and they were working to prove that the pellets from his leg and her car were from the gun. She was being booked into juvenile detention once again, and he was heading there to meet with her and her lawyer and father for an interview. Ben Gordon wouldn't discuss any of the other charges, and Mavis didn't care about them. She didn't even care that Candy was in Juvie, unable to harass her for the time being. All she really cared about was the fact that now she couldn't deal with Candy the way she really wanted to.

While deep in her thoughts, Mavis heard the sound of her parents talking and the front door closing; they were home! She sat up on the edge of her bed, and her eyes immediately met Kim's. Both of them were nervous about telling Jane and Todd about the day's events; they were going to tighten the ropes on Mavis' life that was for sure, even if Candy was locked up.

As if Kim could read her mind, she said, "What are you going to say to them?"

Mavis shrugged, but her thoughts didn't match her nonchalant façade. "I don't know; the truth, I suppose." Her stomach gave a growl, and for the first time, she thought about the fact that Matt wouldn't be working, and therefore couldn't bring her food. She was going to have to hit the liver counter at Flair's.

"Well, are you ready?" Kim asked. "I'm not gonna make you do it alone, girl."

Mavis took a deep breath. "Okay, let's do this thing."

They both stood up, and Mavis stopped at the vanity just long enough to put a little vapor rub under her nose; the last thing she needed right then was to have her growing appetite get the best of her. Together they walked up the hall and turned into the kitchen, where she knew her parents would be chatting while her mother got ready to make supper. As soon as they walked in, both girls stopped and just stood there.

Todd was just opening the daily paper, which he never got to read until late. He looked up at Mavis, and the smile on his face faded immediately. His lack of contribution to whatever conversation he had been having with his wife caught Jane's attention immediately, and she also turned her attention to the girls.

"Hey," Todd started slowly. "Um… why so serious? Bad day?"

Mavis reached out and tugged on Kim's shirtsleeve, indicating that they should sit. Kim got the point, and the girls went to the table and took a couple of chairs. Their persistent silence now had the full attention of Jane and Todd, who hadn't taken their eyes off the girls at all.

"Um… Mom, Dad," Mavis began. "I guess you

could say yes, we sort of had a bad day."

Jane completely forgot about the chicken hindquarters she had out of the fridge. She, too, made her way to the table and took her regular chair. She and Todd exchanged worried glances before speaking in unison, like twins.

"What's wrong?"

Mavis took a deep breath. "Okay, well, it all started when we went to Donnelly for our picnic. We were eating and talking and stuff, and then Matt got shot."

"What?" Once again, the word shot out of their mouths in stereo, and Jane even jumped to her feet, panic all over her face.

Mavis, who was more like her mother than any daughter liked to admit, jumped up as well and held her hands, palms out, in front of her. "No! I mean, yes, he got shot, but he's okay, Mom. It was a pellet gun. I took him to the hospital, they dug it out, gave him a pain pill and antibiotics, and sent him home to rest. I swear he's fine!"

Jane fell into her chair as though every ounce of energy left her body at once. She closed her eyes and put her head back, and the girls could see her chest rising up and down as she struggled to calm down. Kim looked at Mavis and raised her eyebrows, then put her attention on picking at some invisible mark on the table.

Mavis sat back down. "Oh, yeah. My taillight got shot out, too, and the cops had to rip it out for evidence. No biggie."

Now it was Todd's turn to jump to his feet. "They

tore apart your taillight?!"

"Dad! Detective Gordon said the local government will cover it because it was evidentiary!"

Todd collapsed into his chair and put his head in his hand. "You're going to give us both heart attacks…"

Jane sat forward, her overwhelmed look now replaced with grave concern. "Who did this, Mavis? Was it that Wilkes girl?"

She nodded. "Detective Gordon said she has been arrested on multiple charges, including charges for shooting Matt and the car, but others that he wouldn't discuss. She's back in Juvie."

Her parents looked at each other again, this time for several seconds, and Mavis was convinced that the pair were communicating telepathically. Her suspicions seemed to be confirmed when Jane suddenly turned her eyes to Mavis. She looked back at her mother in silence and waited, bracing herself; she didn't have long to wait.

"Please go to the bedroom for a bit, girls," she said quietly. "We need to mull all of this over; it's just about too much to take."

Without speaking, the girls stood up and left the kitchen, and they didn't say another word to each other until the bedroom door was closed behind them. They both sat back down, Kim in the beanbag, Mavis on the bed, and looked at each other.

"Well?" Kim asked in a voice just above a whisper. "What do you think they're gonna do to you?

"To me? Oh, it ain't gonna be just me. You can bet they're gonna be calling your mom and dad, too. I promise you that."

Mavis threw herself back on the bed while Kim groaned loudly. Yes, it had been a crazy day, and it was bound to get crazier. But all they could do was roll with the punches, and hope that it would all come to an end soon.

But Mavis wasn't so sure, because she knew that things could get worse... much worse.

R.W.K. Clark

CHAPTER 22

It wasn't until late that afternoon that Ben Gordon was able to even consider making it down to the Juvenile Detention Center for his interview with Candace Wilkes. Beside his reports; he had to enter the canister, air gun, taillight, and pellets into evidence. Those paper chains were long and tedious every time. He also had to fill out requests for fingerprinting and other lab testing to be done on the items, not to mention the trace that would have to be conducted on the canister to make sure, without a doubt, that it had come from Dr. Michael Hall's former practice. It was a heck of a job, all right.

By the time he actually walked through the double doors with their buzzers and pop locks at Juvie, it was nearly six in the evening. Mr. Wilkes and his attorney, Kenneth Macklin, were waiting in a conference room, both looking frustrated and exhausted. Candy, of course, wasn't there yet; she was having dinner with the other detainees. She would be brought to the meeting upon their request, now that all parties were present.

"My apologies, gentlemen," Ben greeted. "This entire process is costing all of us a lot of time and work. Mr. Macklin, how have you been?"

The man stood and shook his hand before sitting once again. "I think we've all had better days. So, do you want to shoot the details around a bit before we request the presence of our defendant?"

"That's probably a good idea." Ben popped open his briefcase, withdrawing Candy's file and a legal pad and pen. He set them before him neatly, then closed the case. "This is a pretty unfortunate situation, and there is much more to it than simply the charges at hand. First, we have the assault on Matthew Morgan with the pellet gun, as well as the damage that was done to the vehicle belonging to Mavis Harvey. Second, there's the empty nitrous canister belonging to Dr. Michael Hall, which was stolen from his office sometime last fall. I have a witness who can attest to that entire situation; we can go into more detail on that momentarily. Other than that, we have a pretty major case before us that is under investigation which might, or might not, involve Candy, and that case consists of multiple murders." He laced his fingers together, put them casually on top of his legal pad, and smiled at the men across from him. "Where do you want to start?"

Both men were looking at him with their mouths hanging open in disbelief. Ben waited patiently for either of them to say something for several minutes before sitting back in his chair, picking up his pen, and beginning to doodle a bunch of scribbled nonsense on his pad, as if he had nothing better to do. The bluff worked; Kenneth Macklin spoke first.

"Well, let's not get ahead of ourselves here. Let's discuss the active charges first, not the pipe dreams you have in your head."

Ben stopped doodling and smiled again. "Fine. The first two charges consist of the Assault with a Weapon Causing Bodily Injury. Mr. Morgan was shot in the leg with an air rifle pellet gun while picnicking with his girlfriend and another friend at Donnelly Park in Greenville this afternoon. Witnesses saw the perpetrator in the woods before the shooting wearing a red ball cap; the perp was also seen fleeing the scene through the woods just seconds after. When Miss Wilkes' parents were served with a search warrant, she was observed wearing a red ball cap. A pellet gun and pellets were located in the trunk of the family car, which was searched on their return from a family function. Her mother stated that the air rifle had been in the basement for some time and that her daughter must have put it there the night before. At the same time that Mr. Morgan was assaulted, the taillight of Miss Harvey's car was shot out, and both pellets were retrieved for evidence." He paused. "Keep in mind that there has been a long-standing feud between Miss Wilkes and Miss Harvey. Miss Wilkes recently placed a handmade doll resembling Mr. Morgan into Miss Harvey's mailbox with a knife in its chest. She admitted to doing this."

Mr. Wilkes was wringing his hands and staring down at them in disbelief; Kenneth Macklin groaned and sat back in his chair. "Okay, that's a sufficient start, I believe. We can get into more detail later. What about this empty gas canister that was found on the property?"

Ben cleared his throat. "During the fall of last year, Miss Wilkes' best friend, Shanice Hall, threatened a nurse at her father's medical practice. The nurse was coerced to falsify medication inventory for pills and nitrous oxide, which Miss Hall told her she was taking to party with friends. The woman was threatened with her job, and subsequently fired when she accused the physician's daughter of taking possession of the drugs. A nitrous canister was discovered hidden in the Wilkes garage today during the search. It was empty, but it is suspected that this gas was used in the perpetration of the mass murders committed at Westside High in Greenville during the spring of this year. We are currently verifying the origin of the nitrous as being the practice of Dr. Hall, and we are also searching for Shanice Hall. Her family has supposedly left the country and changed their identities. The investigation into their location is ongoing. Unfortunately for Miss Wilkes, she had the empty canister."

Kenneth Macklin was getting red in the face. "I can see the theft of the drug if it is proven to belong to Hall, or at least an accessory charge, but the murders? This is far-fetched, and you have a very long way to go to prove anything when it comes to Candace and any involvement she might have had."

Ben smiled. "That investigation is ongoing. The

charges today are assault causing injury, theft, and possession, and destruction of property. I am simply trying to prepare you for what is to come so that you can give your client a proper defense. Shall we call Candace in now?"

Macklin leaned over and began to whisper into Mr. Wilkes' ear. After a brief moment, Wilkes nodded, but he didn't look encouraging. Ben waited patiently, his smile glued onto his face.

"Detective Gordon, I think it is in the best interest of my client if I confer with them before allowing any sort of interrogation or interview. I'll call you in the morning, after meeting with her, and we can set up a time for all of us to get together and discuss the charges she's facing."

Ben opened his case and began to put his things calmly back inside. "That's completely understandable, considering the magnitude of what she is facing. You have my number, Ken. Mr. Wilkes, here is my card." Ben slid his card across the table to Candy's father, who slowly took it and put it into the breast pocket of his shirt without even glancing at it.

Grabbing his case, Ben stood. "Thank you, gentlemen. I look forward to your call, Ken. Have a good evening."

With that, he walked out of the room, confident in what he had and what he still needed to get in order to close the murders of Jeff Deason, Colin Handley, and most of the junior class of Westside High. He wouldn't let this tragedy go unsolved, and he had a very good feeling he was about to wrap it up.

The rest was really up to Candace Wilkes and what she was willing to take responsibility for.

CHAPTER 23

It was one o'clock in the morning.

Mavis lay in bed, her stomach growling and aching with the lack of satisfaction that the raw liver she had eaten had given her. She missed Matt, and she wished that Kim had spent the night, so she didn't have to be alone. But worst of all was the guilt inside of her; the guilt was far worse than the ravenous hunger, and it kept her from sleeping.

She thought mostly about Matt. She felt that he was in serious danger. Even though she had been tempted by his blood when he was shot, the danger had nothing to do with her. It seemed that Candy Wilkes was off in the head somehow, and her focus of attention was Mavis, though she didn't know why. All she seemed able to sort out in her tired head was that Candy had snapped, and she blamed Mavis for her misery and misdirection. She felt bad for the girl, but at the same time, she was angry and afraid for the boy she cared so much about.

Feeling at the end of her rope, Mavis reached over and grabbed her smartphone, then leaned up on her elbow and fished her earbuds out of the nightstand drawer. Plugging it into the phone by feel, she then buried the buds into her ears and brought up her playlist of music; she didn't need to scroll through to find what she wanted to listen to… she simply let the music play from the beginning of the list.

At first, as the music played, she focused on the words and music, willing it to take her mind off her worries and apprehensions and fears. But by the time the third song rolled around, Mavis finally began to drift off, her mind turning from harsh reality to pleasant dreams, and she fell into a deep sleep. The soft droning of the music kept her there, pleasantly cradling her with its hard beats and meaningful words.

∞

Mavis was standing at Donnelly Park, in the same spot where they had just had their picnic that day, but with some key differences. She was alone, utterly alone, for the park was empty and quiet, except for the chirping of the birds and the slight whistling of the warm breeze in the trees. There was no food basket, no music, and no blanket to sit on. No cars were around, no dogs, no kids… just Mavis and the peace of a worry-free world. She turned to look into the wooded area, which was about ten or fifteen feet from where she stood in the grass; she expected to see the roundness of a head with a cap on it, but there was no one. Relieved, Mavis sat down in the grass and looked to the sky; everything was so bright and colorful, and she could even feel the softness of the grass as she ran her fingers over the surface of the ground.

"Mavis! Mavis, I'm here!"

She turned and looked over her left shoulder, and there he was, Matthew. He looked different somehow; he wasn't dressed in the ripped black jeans that she loved so much, nor did he wear the black t-shirt that he wore so often. No, on this day at Donnelly Park, Matt wore a light blue collared shirt tucked neatly into blue jeans that fit him perfectly. His hair was black, but it was combed in an attractive style, and his eyes were devoid of black liner, his face bare of stark makeup.

He was smiling, and he was walking toward her.

"Don't get up," he told her gently as she began to rise to her feet. "Let's sit together for a while. I want to talk to you."

Mavis settled back into the green grass. She was tempted to lie down, but could not because of her eagerness to see him. Seconds seemed like hours that were merely moments, and then he was sitting beside her. He took her hand, smiled, and kissed her lips.

"Hi," he whispered. "It's so much better here when we're alone, isn't it?"

Even though she knew she could blush no longer, Mavis felt her cheeks redden. "Yes," she replied.

He pointed toward the sky. "Look at how blue it is today… isn't it clear and beautiful?"

Following his direction, Mavis gazed upward. The sun was bright; shining down on everything, eliminating every shadow, and it warmed her cold body. She could even feel her heartbeat once again, though she knew that wasn't possible.

"It's going to be all right, you know. What is meant to happen will happen. Let's walk."

Matt stood, and he took her by the hand and pulled her to her feet. She felt nothing but ecstasy as he held her hand and strolled through the grass with her in silence. Suddenly, she realized that she could feel the grass, every strand, between her toes and on the soles of her feet. Looking down, Mavis realized they were both barefoot. She felt like a child again, unaffected by the harsh realities of life and the world. She glanced at Matt, still taken off guard by his blue jeans; that was when she saw the blood stain on his thigh.

"Don't worry about that," he told her. She looked at him, and he was smiling. "It is the difference between you and me; in the end, we will always be together."

Then, before her very eyes, even as they walked, his black hair began to gray, strand by strand, and small wrinkles were forming on his face, at his mouth, and beneath his eyes. He continued to smile as he aged. His hand became weaker as it held hers, and his step began to falter.

Suddenly, he stopped. Matt reached into his back pocket and pulled out a small, square mirror that had been taken out of its frame. Holding it up to her face, he waited in silence as she looked at her reflection. But she could not see herself, because she wore a black veil.

"You are beautiful to me, no matter what. I will age… you are aged forever. But I will be here. I'm going nowhere, Mavis Harvey…

"And what is supposed to happen, will happen."

CHAPTER 24

Ben Gordon sat at his desk at the Greenville Police Station, typing furiously on his computer as he caught up his notes on the Wilkes case. There were so many details, along with so many gaps, that he had a hard time keeping it all straight. Something about the gaps disturbed him; but even Ben, with ten years of experience as a detective, couldn't put his finger on what that something was. All he knew was that everything he had, and he meant everything was pointing to the missing Shanice Hall and the combative Candace Wilkes being involved with the horrible murders that had rocked the junior class of Westside during the last school year.

He paused; the murders had rocked more than his quaint suburbia, they had rocked the entire city of Toledo. People were still talking, parents were still frightened, and all the gossip told him that some dreaded the upcoming school year. High school kids all over the city were debating whether or not there should be some alternative to homecomings, winter balls, and prom dances. He had a beautiful niece in Cleveland who was talking about skipping her senior prom altogether if the killer in Greenville wasn't caught, and Cleveland was nearly two hours away.

Ben Gordon felt a firm obligation to solve the case, both for his own family and for the people of the city he lived in and loved.

Forcing himself, he continued to type his way through the blank spots and missing clues that he needed to make his case notes complete. The truth was, in his heart, Ben was convinced that Shanice Hall and Candy had developed a severe hatred for Mavis Harvey. He was sure it had happened when Mavis decided to be the one person to ever stand up to the well-to-do, spoiled, self-righteous Shanice. He was also convinced that, at the time of the original bullying incident, Candy was no more than a lowly goombah to Shanice's tormenting behavior when it came to her classmates. But goombah or not, the fact was, she was an accomplice, and she had been found with horribly incriminating evidence when it came to the nitrous canister. Also, she had shot Matthew Morgan in the leg and blown out Mavis' taillight with an air rifle that she had snuck out of her parents' home.

The thoughts in his head motivated him, and his notes began to flow much more smoothly. As he went, he became more and more convinced that he was right: those two girls were responsible for several unnecessary deaths, and he was going to prove it. It excited him to think about closing the case, but more than anything, he wanted to get Candy off the street. Ben was also determined to find Shanice and deal her the same fate, no matter where she was or who her parents were.

Suddenly, Ben's phone rang.

He jumped, then his reflexes made him grab the receiver without a thought. "Detective Gordon, Homicide," he said sternly into the phone.

"Ben, this is Ken Macklin. How's your day?"

Sitting back in his chair, a smile came over his face; he had been waiting for this call. "Hi, Ken. So, what do you have for me? Are you ready to meet and let me have my interview? You know that as a juvenile, Candy can't be arraigned until it's done, so I'm sure her parents are anxious to get the ball rolling. What are you charging them, anyway? Two? Three-hundred an hour?"

The defense attorney ignored his question. "How do you feel about holding the interview tomorrow at ten in the morning? I've met extensively with the girl and her parents, and we feel some kind of agreement can be reached regarding the current charges. We will be pacing ourselves, and have serious reservations when it comes to the craziness you are implying about her involvement with the Greenville murders."

"Ten is fine, Ken." Ben jotted down the time quickly on his desk blotter. "See you then, with bells on."

He didn't wait for a response; Ben Gordon hung up and went back to his typing. This time the gaps and confusion were gone: Ken Macklin's tone of voice said it all. The Wilkes family was nervous, and they were going to take what they could get when it came to the current charges. As for the murder investigation? Well,

Ben was willing to bet that even her loving, concerned, and dedicated parents had their doubts about her innocence at this point.

Ben paused and reached behind him to his bookshelf, which held his small stereo on the top shelf. He turned up the volume on his favorite country and western station and began to type to the music. This was going to wrap up nicely. Maybe too nice, but it needed to wrap up, and there needed to be no loose ends. He didn't like loose ends… never had, never would.

∞

The dream of Matt and her walking in the park remained sharp in her mind, and she felt comfort and peace, knowing that what would be, would be. Mavis slept so deeply that she almost didn't wake to the sound of her cell phone ringing at nine the next morning. Her ringtone was blaring from her phone, and she almost missed the call. During the last few notes of the ring, her groping hand found her phone buried under her right shoulder.

"Hello?"

The wonderful sound of Matt's voice, a bit slurred and tired, but happy, came over the line.

"Mav? Hey, babe! I almost thought you weren't going to answer for a minute. Good morning!"

Mavis sat up straight in her bed, her head clearing fast. "Matthew? I thought about you, and I dreamed about you, all night! It's so good to hear your voice!" Even in her sleepy state, Mavis was almost ready to cry with relief.

"I'm here, Mavis," he said soothingly. "I'll always be here. How are you feeling?"

She broke out in laughter. How was she feeling? He was the one who got hurt! It was just like Matt to worry more about her than himself; she loved him so much! She collapsed backward into her pillow and wiped at her teary, sleepy eyes.

"I dreamed of you," she said softly.

Matt moaned. "Was it good, or was it bad?"

"It was good. It was so good. But I've missed you."

He chuckled, but Mavis could tell that he was feeling the after-effects of the pain medication. "Aw, you're just missing my awesome cooking, aren't you?"

"Funny," she replied lightly; it was a good joke. "Actually, Kim and I made a trip to Flair's, and I picked up some juicy liver. Kind of reminded me of old times, but I have to admit, your food is definitely the best. So, enough about me… how are you feeling? You're the one who got shot."

Matt gave a macho groan and said in a John Wayne voice, "I'm feelin' like a cowboy, lady."

"You are a cowboy."

They laughed together, then Matt's voice got serious. "So, you haven't really said how you're feeling. I know you, and I know that you're having a hard time with all of this, mostly for your own reasons. But I want you to see that this is going to come out all right. My mother woke me and told me that she got a call from that detective, and he told her that Candy was arrested and they found the pellet gun she shot me with. She's got a bunch of charges, and they believe she was involved with the murders because of some kind of evidence they found in her parents' garage."

"But she didn't do the murders, Matt," Mavis muttered, closing her eyes in frustration. "This is why I have a hard time with all of this. I mean, besides the fact that she obviously wants to hurt you because of me. I know they want to pin them on her, but she didn't do them, and that's just not right."

Matt sighed loudly. "Mavis, if you are having such a hard time with this, then go to the detective and confess. Tell him you're a zombie and that you ate them all in the heat of the moment. He's going to think you're crazy! You probably won't even go to prison, they'll just lock you up in some psychiatric hospital for the rest of your life with people that think they're really Napoleon or Joan of Arc. They'll dope you up until you spend the rest of your days slobbering on yourself, and the rest of your days could last forever, in your condition."

He paused, and Mavis remained quiet. "Look," he said finally. "It would be different if you had killed Jeff and Colin and the others out of malice. Then you'd be nothing more than a cold-blooded, cannibalistic killer, like Jefferey Dahmer or someone. But you are not. You are just Mavis, a girl that something unexplainable is happening to that no one can possibly understand. There might be a morally right way to handle this, but until we can think of it without compromising your existence, well, I think we have to go with the flow on this one and let things happen the way they are going to happen."

He was right. Everything he was telling her was true. She hadn't meant to kill anyone, much less eat them, and this was the way to deal with it for now. She had to snap out of it; she had to put one foot in front of the other. Besides, it appeared that Candy Wilkes did want to kill him, or at least hurt him. She certainly wanted to frighten Mavis and get back at her for the trouble last fall, and she had proven that by her actions at Donnelly Park and more.

"Okay," she finally said. "I'm going to pull myself together."

"Good," Matt replied, obviously relieved. "Now, I have to work tonight, so at some point today I am going to get more sleep, but do you have what you need right now? I mean, food-wise, that is?"

She made an agreeable sound. "I'll be fine. Take care of you."

"Make sure to use your vapor rub," he stated firmly. "After yesterday, it's very clear to me that we can't be lax with that, especially since I haven't been able to get you what you need."

"I will."

The two chatted a bit longer, made plans to see each other the following day, and then hung up. Mavis lay in bed for a little while longer, until her mother was knocking at her door, telling her to get up and eat. Her stomach was growling, and even though she knew her breakfast wouldn't be anything she craved, she complied willingly, even happily.

After all, if she was going to take things a step at a time, she had to take the first step.

CHAPTER 25

Candy Wilkes walked into the conference room at the juvenile detention center, escorted by a female staff member in a brown uniform.

"I'll be right outside the door if there are any problems," the woman told the group seated at the table. "Are you comfortable with her restraints being removed, or would you prefer they be left on?"

Ben Gordon looked at the Wilkeses and Kenneth Macklin, all of whom were looking to him for the answer; he certainly didn't care if they took off her cuffs. The girl was all of five-foot-four and a hundred twenty pounds. Ben was pretty sure he could overcome the girl if he had to.

"You can remove them," he told the woman.

She complied, then stepped out of the room. Candy sat down in the chair, right between her parents. She rubbed her wrists for a moment while her mother tried to plant a kiss on her cheek. Candy jerked away from her and made a face. The girl had such an attitude. Ben was beginning to think her problems were far deeper than criminal; it seemed she was an emotional and mental basket case.

"Candace, we love you, and we're trying to help you," Larry Wilkes said gently, but the girl didn't acknowledge him.

Ken Macklin spoke first. "Well, we all know why we're here. This is the police interview for the charges of Assault Causing Bodily Injury, Destruction of Property, and Theft. You understand this, don't you Candy?"

The girl held her eyes firmly on the table in front of her and nodded.

"Fine," the attorney said, frustration tinging his voice. "Go ahead, Ben."

With paper and pen ready, Ben began to ask his questions. "So, Candy, you know what evidence we found at your home, and you are aware of all prior circumstances leading up to the search and your arrest. I take it we don't have to go over any of that again, am I correct?"

"Yep."

Ben sat back. "So, do you want to tell me what you did?"

"You know what I did, you just said it."

He took a breath. "Well, if the prosecutor is going to have leniency in offering a plea that won't put you in adult court or jail, we need to hear you take responsibility by telling us your story, do you understand?"

"Fine," she replied.

"Start at the beginning, Candy," Macklin said simply. "Just like we talked about. Cooperation is the most important thing here."

The girl took a breath. "Okay. Last fall, there was a situation at school with me and my best friend Shanice pushing this girl around in the bathroom. Mavis Harvey came in and got in the middle of it. This made us mad, and we decided she needed to learn a lesson, so later we jumped her when she was going home from the grocery store. We didn't win the fight, but because we attacked her, we got arrested and had to go to Juvie."

Candy's voice was flat and dead, just like her eyes, but at least she was talking and telling Ben what he needed to hear.

"Go on," he urged.

"Well, this trouble made Shanice's dad have problems, so they moved to Cleveland, which wasn't too bad because she came to see me a couple of times, and we talked on the phone a lot. Anyway, we were both still mad, even more then, because she had to move away. We joked about getting Mavis back someday, but whatever. Anyway, the next thing I knew, Shanice was gone, and I haven't seen her since. It makes me angry, and I wanted to get back at Mavis, freak her out. So, I made the stupid doll and put it in the mailbox, which I got in trouble for, for harassing her. Whatever."

The group waited for her to continue, watching her closely during her pause. She had started picking at her fingernails, and now a small smile was pulling at the corners of her mouth. Ben couldn't be sure why, but he knew it was her enjoying her memories of these incidents.

"My parents took me out of school and all that anyway," she continued. "I can never leave the house, and I have no friends. My entire life is over, and it's all her fault, so I wanted her to be miserable too. I got my dad's pellet gun out of the basement and put it in the car before the reunion. I had been pranking her on the phone, and I planned to go to her house and shoot out some windows. The only time I could get away was to sneak, so I talked my cousin into taking the little kids to Donnelly to play. While I was sneaking through the park to go to her house, I saw her and her friends through the trees. It was perfect, so I shot at them."

"Did you intend to hurt the boy?" Ben asked.

Candy shrugged, smiling now. "No, but I'm glad I did."

Ben was writing furiously. "So, you are admitting to the shooting. What about the empty nitrous canister?"

"That was left over from Shanice," she said, her smile fading. "She used to go to her dad's office and get pills and canisters, and we would get high with a couple of our friends. That was the last canister, which we used up at my house. I just hid it because I didn't know what else to do with it; she never told me, and by then she was gone."

Ben believed her, thanks to the story Jessica Reynolds, Dr. Hall's former nurse, told him. "That's believable, that you didn't steal it. I have some other questions about the nitrous, but I can say that the prosecutor will likely drop the theft down to a Possession of Stolen Property charge; that helps."

Candy looked up. "So, ask your other questions so I can be done with this, please."

Ben raised his eyebrows. "Okay. Where were you on the night of the homecoming dance last year?"

Candy glanced at her parents, then looked down at her hands. "I was with Shanice. She had taken her mom's car; her mom was passed out drunk. We cruised around most of the night, and since we had just gotten out of juvie, we wanted to hang out."

"At any point that night did you run into Jeffrey Deason?" Ben watched her face closely.

"Nope."

He narrowed his eyes. "Not at all? Didn't cruise by the school for the game, or to go into the dance, not once?"

"Nope. Just hung out."

Ben wrote; she wasn't going to admit to more on that one, not right then. He was going to have to find more evidence on her if he was going to charge her for Jeff's death. He'd be sure to stay on it.

"What about the night of the Winter Formal? Where were you then?"

Candy glanced up at him. "I was alone, at home." She gave both of her parents a glance, then looked away. "They were out with friends, I didn't have a date, and Shanice wasn't able to come from Cleveland, so I watched a movie."

"Did you call, see, or speak with Colin Handley on that night?"

"Nope."

Ben focused his eyes on her again, looking for any guilty reaction. "Did you leave home at any point and go to his house?"

"I said no, didn't I?"

He went back to writing; he'd keep working on the proof for Colin, too. "Okay. Now, tell me about Junior Prom."

Candy looked right at him and smiled, her eyes even lighting up. "What about it?"

"Did you go?"

She continued to look at him and smile. "My parents don't let me breathe, much less go to a dance. By that time, I was being held prisoner at home."

He didn't believe her. "Did the nitrous canister have anything to do with it?"

"With what?" she asked.

"Prom, Candy."

She kept smiling but looked back down at her hands. "I already answered you about prom."

Ben knew that he wasn't going to get anything out of her about the murders, at least, not that day. "Okay. Well, I guess we have what we need for the charges at hand. I need you to write down the details on the incident at the park, and about the canister, for a confession. This allows the prosecutor to have the freedom to work with you when it comes to charges and sentencing. The more you cooperate, the better your chances of having easier consequences, do you understand?"

Candy nodded.

Ben slid a pad of statement sheets and a pen across the table at the girl, she took it and began to write. He watched her for a brief moment; she was still smiling, and it gave him the creeps. The girl was sick, and they all knew it. He turned his attention to Ken Macklin.

"Ken, I'll be questioning Candy in the future regarding the prom incident, and more than likely the Deason and Handley murders as well. I think we both know she has more information than she is sharing." He turned his gaze back to her, and she looked up at him and smirked sarcastically before continuing with her confession.

"So, we're done here for now?" Macklin asked.

Ben nodded. "As you know, the juvenile prosecutor will be in touch with you so Candy can be arraigned and a plea can be reached."

The group sat there in silence until the girl was finished, then the two attorneys left while the Wilkeses stayed to visit with their daughter. The men went their separate ways to tend to the business at hand.

As Ben drove, he thought about the murder cases. He knew that she would likely not cop to any of it, and it seemed that condemning evidence was non-existent when it came to the case. If he was going to get her for anything, it was going to be connected to the canister. Ben Gordon was sure that it was used to overtake the prom-goers, but to know for sure he had to get it out of the girl.

She would be seeing him again soon.

CHAPTER 26

That same morning, while Candy was in the middle of her interview with Detective Gordon and the others, Mavis sat at the table with her mother. It was the first time the two actually had to sit and talk alone together in a couple of weeks since all of the chaos had started. For Mavis, it felt good to just be with Jane. They had always been so close, and even though they lived together, she missed her mom. A plate of bacon, eggs, and toast sat before her, along with a cold glass of milk. Mavis took dutiful bites now and then, enough to fill her stomach, even if it didn't satisfy her growing zombie appetite.

"Do you feel better knowing that Candy is locked up?" Jane asked. "I know I do."

Mavis nodded. "Yeah, I guess. I mean, it's hard to feel good about this sort of thing, but I guess I'm a bit relieved. I feel bad for her in a lot of ways, though."

"How? Why?"

After swallowing the bite she had just taken, she sat back in her chair, thought about her words, and replied, "Well, when all things are considered, I guess I feel compassion. Kim pointed out to me the other day that the girl has been a follower all through school. After the assault last fall, she lost her best friend, and then her parents shut her up and didn't let her have a life, or make any new ones. I guess I feel partly responsible." She picked her fork back up and took another bite of her eggs.

Jane sat back in her chair and crossed her arms over her chest. "You know, dear, that's one way to look at it. But let's look at it from another perspective, shall we? Take you and Kim, for instance. Both of you have been friends forever; you're like sisters. You have good souls and similar interests, though, in reality, you don't have much in common as people. What you do have in common is the way you think and how your hearts respond to the world around you, wouldn't you agree?"

Mavis nodded.

"Okay, then. In my experience, it is the heart that draws two people together." Jane paused and took a drink of her coffee. "I believe, as does Detective Gordon, that Shanice Hall just has an ugly heart. Consider for a moment, the fact that the ugliness in her might have been attracted to an ugliness inside of Candy Wilkes. If that were the case, then something in Candy is no good as well."

"But her parents…"

Jane held up her hand. "I know what you're going to say. She isn't spoiled, they are religious, and they've done the best they can to discipline her and teach her right from wrong. I think that proves my point. Even after Shanice left and went wherever she went. Candy still chose to make decisions that were harmful to others. Do you understand what I'm trying to say? She is responsible for her choices, just as you are. Look, as you get older, you and Kim see less and less of each other. She is getting closer to Shawn, and now they are planning a future. You have Matt. People change, and they grow apart, but you aren't running over to Shawn's house and putting bloody dolls in the mailbox, or trying to shoot him in the leg."

Mavis thought about her mother's words; she was right. Even though Mavis knew that she had been the one to kill Jeff and Colin, and even caused the deaths at prom, the situation at hand was different. She was not responsible for Candy's situation in the slightest.

"But what if she gets into trouble for all those murders, and she didn't do it?" Her mother gave her a confused look, and Mavis quickly added, "I mean, I just can't see Candy being smart enough, or tricky enough, to do those things, especially since Shanice is gone. Shanice was always the instigator… the main conspirator, everyone knows that."

Jane nodded. "Well, dear, I guess you will have to trust the police to come to conclusions based on the evidence they find. You'll have to trust the courts to do the right thing. Right now, at this moment in time, she is in trouble for nothing other than what we know she has done. That's where we are today. Listen, I know you still hurt over the boys, even with Matt in your life. You might hurt your entire life, but you can't blame yourself."

Little did her mother know, she certainly could.

"When have you and Dad talked to Detective Gordon?"

Jane smiled at her daughter. "Several times; he has kept us posted. As a matter of fact, he called me this morning to let me know that Candy filled out a confession for the assault, among other things. I am your mother, you know. It is my job to keep tabs and to know what's going on. Now, eat your breakfast, okay?"

"Okay."

Jane got up and started the dishwater in the sink. Mavis watched her while she ate, but her mind was still on Candy. She was going to have to let it go, but how? What could she do to get her own guilt out of her head?

She wasn't sure, but for now, she was going to start by focusing on helping her mother clean the kitchen. She cleared her plate, took it to the sink, and got busy. The best thing she could do was put her mind on other things, and she could simply do it second by second, minute by minute.

∞

Ben Gordon was once again at his computer, tapping away in an effort to finish up the reports on Candy Wilkes' charges so he could get them to the prosecutor. As his fingers flew over his keyboard, his phone suddenly rang. He jumped, groaned, and plucked up the receiver, frustrated by the interruption.

"Gordon," he said into the phone.

"Detective, this is Carol from the Evidence Lab. Sounds like I pulled you away from something." The woman sounded amused; she had worked with him for years, and she knew the sound of his voice when he was busy. "This might make you feel better: I have results on the nitrous container from the case you're working on."

Ben sat back in his chair. "Shoot."

"Okay, the lot number allowed me to definitively trace it back to an order placed by a Dr. Michael Hall, who used to have a practice here in Greenville." She paused briefly. "Though, it does appear he is no longer in practice, here or in any other state."

Ben started to write on his pad. "Right, we're aware of that. Is that all?"

"No, there's more," she continued. "We have several sets of prints that we were able to lift off the container; four, to be exact. One goes back to a shipping clerk at the pharmaceutical company that produced the gas; another traced to a woman who used to be a nurse for Dr. Hall. She submitted her prints to the medical association when she was licensed, but she has no criminal record to speak of, so I think her prints can be explained. There were two more matches: a juvenile named Shanice Hall… she might be related to the doctor. Perhaps she helped with the shipment when it arrived?"

"I'm aware of why her prints would be on there," Ben stated. "The fourth?"

"A Candace Wilkes, the defendant in your case."

Ben stopped writing and sat back. "These are things I expected, but needed, nonetheless. Great work, thank you."

He was getting ready to hang up when Carol's voice stopped him. "Wait, Ben, there's one more thing: the canister's nozzle was manually tampered with, though I'm not sure why. It appears that the needle inside was intentionally snapped off. The prints found on and around the nozzle were those of Miss Wilkes."

Ben froze. "Well, wouldn't they have to snap the needle to use the gas to get high?"

"No, the needle inside the nozzles of canisters of this type are designed in a manner that permits the release of gas with slight bending; that's what the hose contraptions and face masks are designed to do, while still permitting the needle to go back into its original position. This allows for the use of the canister with multiple patients, do you see what I mean?"

"Could it have snapped off by accident?" he asked.

"Again, no," Carol replied. "These things are made tough; they have to be to ensure the safety of others in its vicinity during use. Also, it was a clean break, meaning it was done all at once, not over time, by continuous bending from prolonged use. In my opinion, the needle was snapped intentionally."

"Why would someone do that?"

Carol sighed. "To release the gas all at once. Now, perhaps your defendant was paranoid about having it full in her possession, or maybe she was just farting around and released it all into the air to watch the tweeting birdies go to La-La Land? But in the few past cases, I've researched, this has been done when the gas is intentionally being used in a situation of submission and control."

Ben was elated. "Thank you, Carol. I love you, lady."

"Well, I can't say the same in return, but you're welcome."

Ben hung up the phone, then immediately picked it up and dialed the number for Ken Macklin.

"Macklin."

Clearing his throat, Ben said with a smile. "Ken, I'm going to need to meet with you and your client as soon as possible. Looks like she has a little more trouble on her hands than she realizes."

R.W.K. Clark

CHAPTER 27

Candy Wilkes, her mother, Ken Macklin, and Ben Gordon all sat in the detention conference room once again. This time, they were meeting to discuss the new evidence that Carol from the lab had presented to him on the telephone regarding the nitrous canister. Ben was confident that he had the girl against the wall with this one, definitely on the prom attack, anyway. He hoped that she would crumble and confess to all the murders, but regardless of the outcome, he had presented the new evidence to the juvenile prosecutor, and Candy was being charged with several counts of Homicide… 2nd Degree, for the time being, whether she copped to the charges or not.

"I think I'll begin today," Ben started, a satisfied smile on his face. "Candy, did your attorney explain to you why we're here again so soon?"

The girl sat in her chair, rocking back and forth rhythmically. She had seen the detention psychiatrist that morning, and now she was being given medications for mild sedation and bipolar disorder. Ben was glad, but he felt they were a day late and a dollar short; if this had been done before none of these things would have probably happened. Now, it was just too late.

"Candy, did you hear the detective's question?" Ken asked.

She gave a half-chuckle. "I'm being charged with killing the prom."

"Well, the people at the prom, anyway," Ben replied. "We discovered that you snapped the needle off from the canister nozzle, and that is usually done when one is trying to fill a room with gas. Would you like to explain to me why you did that?"

Candy paused, a look of confusion on her face, then replied, "To make my mom and dad sleep."

"Your mom and dad?" Ben was incredulous. As a matter of fact, he was amused at her creativity. "Why would you do that?"

"So, I could go out, duh! They never let me go anywhere!"

"Where did you go, Candy?" Ben knew what she was going to say before she said it.

The girl laughed. "The prom, but now they're all dead."

He sat back in his chair and looked at Ken, who had his hand on his forehead in grief. "So, are you saying you did the prom killings?"

"They were dead when I got there."

Ben began to write on his pad. "Candy, it would help you a lot if you would just be honest about what you did." He looked over at Mrs. Wilkes, who was sobbing silently into a handkerchief. "Mrs. Wilkes, do you remember any situation from last spring when your daughter might have gassed you? For instance, do you recall any evening that your mind simply can't pull up? Spaces in time, or lapses in the order of events from around that time?"

The woman let out a whimper and shook her head vigorously.

Ben turned back to Candy, who was now staring at him vacantly, a partial smile on her face. "Honesty is your only friend right now. You should tell her, Ken."

The attorney looked at his client, then leaned over and whispered in her ear. Ben overheard him ask, "Candy, did you kill any of the victims at prom? Just whisper the answer into my ear."

Ken Macklin turned his ear to the half-dazed girl so she could respond, and that was when she snapped.

"Killed them all! Killed them all! All of them are dead!" Candy screamed it so loudly into his ear that Ken shot back hard into his chair, hand to his pained ear and nearly fell backward onto the floor.

Jumping out of her chair, the girl continued to screech. "The hell with you! All of you! You to mother, everyone is dead, dead, dead!"

The door to the conference room flew open, and a female guard flew inside, followed by two males. A struggle ensued as they tried to gain control of the insane girl, but even though there were three of them, she got the best of them at first. After fighting her for several minutes, with Mrs. Wilkes cowering and crying in a corner out of fear and grief, they were able to cuff and shackle her, even wrapping her in buckling leather restraints. The two men picked up the screaming Candy Wilkes, who was now blubbering to Shanice Hall to get her out of there, that it was all her fault.

"I'm sorry," said the panting, sweating female guard. "You all are going to have to resume this when she is in a clearer state."

She left the room in a rush, and Ken Macklin ran to Mrs. Wilkes to help her up. "Doris, I don't want you to worry; we are going to deal with this."

The woman was nodding while she cried, wiping at her face with the now-soaked hanky. "I have to leave; I have to get Larry and tell him what she has done." She turned to Ben. "I am so sorry, Detective. I could not be sorrier."

"Doris, don't say another word," Ken stated firmly. "I don't want you to drive in this state. Wait for me out in the lobby. I'll take you to Larry's office when we're done here."

After Doris Wilkes left the room, both Ken and Ben took deep breaths. Ben sat down hard in his chair; he was both disturbed and elated. He felt sorry for the teen but sorrier for the junior class of Westside High. He felt anger, and he felt pity. Most of all, he was motivated.

"You know, Ken, this is only the beginning," he said to the attorney. "I'm going to be seeking to charge her with two more counts."

Ken Macklin nodded. "I understand your position, but I will be working to have her confession thrown out. I also understand the weight of the canister evidence, however." He reached out and shook Ben's hand; they both knew it was all in a day's work. "We'll see where the road takes us."

When Ken Macklin left the conference room, Ben sat alone for a long time. At first, he just sat frozen in silence, reliving the events of the last fifteen minutes over and over in his mind. Then he reached in his suit coat pocket and pulled out his own handkerchief. He wiped his forehead and the back of his neck.

Then, Detective Ben Gordon of the Greenville Police Department's Homicide Division broke down in a flood of exhausted tears of his own.

R.W.K. Clark

EPILOGUE

Two Months Later

The Harvey family and those close to them were getting on with their lives.

In the bright summer sun of the beautiful August day: Kim, Matt, and Mavis sat in the grass in the backyard, laughing and playing with Feisty. Her parents and Grandma Cabot sat on the patio in the shade, drinking iced tea and chatting. Todd grilled steaks on the barbecue with Shawn and paid special attention to Mavis' steak. It was important that hers be rare.

Matt got up to help Jane get the side dishes from inside the house, and Kim went up to the patio for a soda and to chat with Grandma Cabot about the growing wedding plans she had with Shawn for after graduation. Mavis remained in the grass. She watched everyone laughing, happy and at peace, and she was thankful.

Lying down in the grass, she let the sun warm her face, and she thought about the events of the last couple of months. All of it still caused a twinge of pain inside of her, but overall, she was getting over it. She was getting better and better at "living" with her condition, and she was learning that being a zombie wasn't so bad.

Candy Wilkes came to her mind. The girl was currently held at the Greenville Psychiatric Hospital for the Criminally Insane. She had received consecutive life sentences, to be served at the hospital, until such a time that doctors believed she was of sound enough mind to be transferred to the women's prison. She had been charged as an adult. As far as Detective Gordon had told them, she was out of her mind, and it looked like she would be at the hospital for some time to come. He continued to work on the murders of Jeff and Colin, determined to find enough evidence to charge Candy for them as well. He also continued to search for Shanice Hall, who he believed orchestrated everything.

Mavis wasn't going to hold her breath; something in her heart told her that the cases were both going to grow ice cold. It didn't make her happy, but in a way, it made her feel safe and secure. She would be fine.

Matt had brought up the subject of getting married after graduation recently, too. While Mavis thought it was too good to be true, and very much wanted to accept, she told him she would rather he ask her again after they finished school. She wanted him to be sure of what he would be getting into by marrying a zombie. It was essential that he did not commit without a solid understanding that this would never end. They would always be scrambling to keep her from hurting others. Matt thought it would be adventurous and fun. Mavis, on the other hand, wasn't so sure. She told him, simply, that it was best if they wait. If he really loved her, he would still love her at the end of senior year.

Senior year was just around the corner; it would start in a few weeks. Time to focus on studies, finals, SATs, and think about college. Time to decide for sure what she wanted to do with her life (or walking death). Time to realize that living at home with mom and dad was soon to be a memory. In many ways, she was scared; in some ways, she couldn't wait.

"Mavis, let's chow down!"

She turned to look at her people, all at the table on the patio, waiting for her to join them. They were all giving her expectant, if not impatient, smiles, and she couldn't help but smile, too. Sitting up, she got to her feet and started walking toward them. From clear across the yard, she could smell her bloody steak, and she thought of the pig brains Matt had brought her for breakfast. She found herself wishing she could have them now, even though the steak smelled great.

Yeah, Mavis thought as she reveled in the feeling of the grass on her feet, things are going to be fine.

∞

Ben Gordon steered his car in the direction of home, exhausted, satisfied, and looking forward to work on Monday. Then, he would be continuing to find whatever there was to find that would put Candy at the Deason and Handley murder scenes. For now, she was locked up but good, and that would do. He could relax, spend time with his family, and go a little easier on himself.

What a strange case, he thought as he pulled onto

the freeway exit. That poor Wilkes girl had really fallen apart, but it hadn't happened overnight. He believed firmly that she had been a bad seed for a very long time, maybe even from the start. It was just too bad that people had to die as a result.

His mind shifted to the murder trial. Candy had sat through the entire thing, pretty much drooling on herself and mumbling nonsense. Ken Macklin had allowed it to go just so far before changing the plea to not guilty by reason of insanity, thinking that would help. But the people of Greenville still had open wounds, and it was a bit too late. It also didn't help that, on the day he changed the plea, Candy stood up in court and began ranting about blood and guts. The judge wouldn't accept the plea, and she was found guilty. The only mercy she was shown was when she was sent to the hospital to get help before doing her time. In a way, he hoped she never left the hospital. Even if she came out of her insanity, she would never likely be able to handle prison life; she should probably stay right where she was.

He had met with her parents after her sentencing. Ben knew they loved her and had done everything they could. But in the end, Larry and Doris Wilkes knew right from wrong, and they believed she needed to be locked up. It hurt them, but even as he spoke with them and tried to encourage them, he saw relief on their faces, and he heard it in their voices. They were glad the nightmare of dealing with their own beloved daughter was over.

Ben still had no idea where Shanice Hall and her family were. At one point in July, he thought he had tracked them to Switzerland, but the lead was a dead end. He also attempted to try to talk to several members of Aneta Hall's extended family, but none of them were willing to spill any beans at all. Everyone he talked to referred to her and her husband and daughter in the past-tense. Foreigners, he thought; they could be such a jerk when it came to their loyalty, even when that loyalty was totally undeserved.

All those people, dead and missed. Young, high school-aged loved ones and teachers who were mangled and mutilated. What was it all for? Revenge? It seemed far-fetched, but in the mind of a sick, twisted seventeen-year-old girl, it had all been justified. Did Shanice think her behavior was warranted as well? He was sure she did. He couldn't wait to get his hands on that one, and he would deal with her father as well. Ben firmly believed that her parents were to blame for all of it, those enabling, self-centered people.

Then he thought of Mavis. She hadn't deserved anything she had gotten. He hoped that everything turned out all right for her. He hoped that she would learn to live with the pain of her losses and move on. Ben was sure that she would.

Pulling into his driveway, Ben turned off his car and just sat for a moment, looking at his home. He needed to mow the grass, and he knew the garage needed cleaning. Well, he had his weekend cut out for him. Getting out of the car, he made his way up the walk and into the house, where supper was on the table, and his family waited.

Yes, everything was right in Greenville, Ohio… for now.

ENTREATY

This book was made possible by reviews from readers like you. Reviews fuel my creativity. If you enjoyed this novel, I implore you to please write a review and share your experience on the retailer's website. The livelihood for authors is entirely dependent on reviews, and I must say, it is the largest obstacle as a struggling author that I have encountered. Please tell a friend, tell a loved one about this read. With your help, I will be one step closer to overcoming this obstacle. In return, I thank you from the bottom of my heart, and sincerely appreciate your time and effort.

Humbled, with gratitude,

R.W.K. Clark

ABOUT THE AUTHOR

I am a father of two beautiful children, Jon and Kim. They are my motivating forces; they are the lighthouse in this vast ocean. In my life, they are the air that I breathe; they are the oasis in this desert of uncertainty. They are my greatest joy in life and my number one priority. I have a long list of hobbies, and I attribute that to my lust for life! I like to surround myself with positive people, who share the same interests. Family values, the arts, outdoors, nature, and travel are tops on my list. I embrace attending cultural and artistic events because I believe dramatic self-expression is the window to the soul. I wear my heart on my sleeve, and I still believe in chivalry, and I always treat people the way I want to be treated.

www.rwkclark.com